NO TRUE ECHO

NO TRUE ECHO

by

GARETH P. JONES

AMULET BOOKS
NEW YORK

Library of Congress Cataloging-in-Publication Data
Jones, Gareth P.
No true Echo / Gareth P. Jones.
pages cm
ISBN 978-1-4197-0784-1 (hardback) — ISBN 978-1-61312-486-4 (ebook)
[1. Time travel—Fiction. 2. Mothers—Fiction. 3. Science fiction.] I. Title.
PZ7.J712No 2015
[Fic]—dc23
2015006549

Text copyright © 2015 Gareth P. Jones
Jacket photography copyright © 2015 WIN-Initiative/Getty Images;
Ron Evans/ Photolibrary/Getty Images
Book design by Maria T. Middleton

First published in Great Britain by Hot Key Books in 2015.

Printed and bound in U.S.A.
10 9 8 7 6 5 4 3 2 1

Amulet Books are available at special discounts when purchased in quantity for premiums and promotions as well as fundraising or educational use. Special editions can also be created to specification. For details, contact specialsales@abramsbooks.com or the address below.

115 West 18th Street
New York, NY 10011
www.abramsbooks.com

For

PATRICK YARKER

and

NICOLA FURNEAUX,

two inspirational teachers

I have an affection for it, for
it was the offspring of happy days,
when death and grief were but words,
which found no true echo in my heart.

MARY SHELLEY on *Frankenstein*

CHAPTER 1

THE NATIONAL MUSEUM OF ECHO TECHNOLOGY

SINCE THE TRIAL, LIPHOOK HAD FOUND HERSELF FEELing increasingly nostalgic. She didn't like it. All the other pensioners on the coach might have been content to natter on about the old days, but Liphook had never been interested in looking back.

Only now that her memories were shifting and twisting did it feel important to try to cling to the truth. A part of her hoped that by remembering, she would be able to make it more real.

She stared out at the lush landscape of Wellcome Valley. It had always bored her. The coach followed the winding valley road, passing rolling hills, tall trees, and fast-flowing rivers.

All of it so very dull.

"You have arrived at the National Museum of Echo

Technology," said the electronic announcement when the coach pulled into the car park.

Liphook waited for all the old people to shuffle off before standing up and making her way along the aisle. Every step hurt.

"Do you need a hand, love?" asked the driver.

"I'm fine," she replied quickly. She didn't want the driver's sympathy. She climbed off the coach and prayed that her legs didn't give up on her and justify his concerns. The doctors had recommended walking with a stick. All that technology at their disposal and that's all they could suggest. A stick. Liphook refused to walk with a stick.

By the time she reached the edge of the car park, the other pensioners were already in the queue at the bottom of the steps. She recalled how different it had been when she had first visited the place. There had been a field where the car park now stood. The trees that lined the field had been chopped down and steps built where there had been a slope. During the trial, she had explained how one of the rainiest months since records began had made the slope muddy and treacherous, but now when she tried to bring it to mind, she couldn't even remember what month it had been.

"Can I help you?" The enthusiastic young man wore a bright orange T-shirt with the logo of an arrow doubling back on itself to form a globe. "There's an escalator a little further along."

"I'm fine." Liphook went to step down, but her leg wobbled and her body lurched forward. With no handrail, she would have fallen if the young man hadn't caught her. He was stronger than he looked. Or she was lighter than she realized.

"Thank you," she muttered.

"Please, I'm supposed to look busy," said the young man. "Would you mind letting me walk down with you? Otherwise they'll have me picking up rubbish again."

Liphook nodded and held out her arm, but her pride prevented her from acknowledging his kindness. Slowly they made their way down the steps together.

"Have you come far today?" asked the man.

"It feels like a long way, yes," said Liphook. "You live here in the valley, do you?"

"Yes. It's beautiful this time of year."

"It won't last."

The man caught her eye but found no indication that she was joking. Liphook had always hated Wellcome Valley, even during the summer months when she first arrived.

By the time they reached the bottom, Liphook was out of breath. *Pathetic old woman,* she thought. *Defeated by a flight of stairs.* At the bottom of the steps, she looked at the queue snaking around the side of the building.

"Will it take long?" she asked.

"Oh, that's the queue for the general public," said the young man. "Special guests like you can go straight in."

For a moment, Liphook wondered if he had recognized her, but from the way he winked she understood that he was being kind again.

"Thank you," she said. As a police officer, she had been used to jumping queues, so she felt no embarrassment about it.

She sat down on a bench inside the museum while the young man purchased her ticket.

"Would you like me to accompany you?" he asked when he returned. "After all, I am here to help." He turned around, revealing the back of his T-shirt with the words *Any Questions?* "Is there any specific reason for your visit today?"

"I've been here before," said Liphook.

"Well, you'll find we've got a lot of new features. The aim is to keep up with technology and ensure that the museum stays relevant."

"It's hard to stay relevant," she replied before accepting the man's help to stand. Together they went through a door into a room full of scientific equipment. The hologram of an annoyingly cheerful woman greeted them.

"Hello," it said. "Welcome to the Discovery Room, where Professor David Maguire created the first time particle accelerator, also known as an echo—"

"Can you turn that off?" interrupted Liphook grumpily.

The hologram vanished.

"Sorry," said the man. "So, this room has been recreated exactly as it would have been when Professor Maguire was working here."

"It looks different to me," said Liphook.

"Really? Because I've seen footage and I think they've done an amazing job," said the young man.

"It's not the same," said Liphook.

"When exactly did you come here?"

"Before it was a museum," replied Liphook.

The young man looked at her with renewed interest. "What's different?" he asked. "I'm sure our experts would love to speak to an actual eyewitness. They're always looking for ways to make it more authentic."

"As I recall, there was more blood," said Liphook.

CHAPTER 2

SCARLETT WHITE

IT WAS ANOTHER MISERABLE DAY IN THE VALLEY. THE sky was so dark that I wondered if the sun had bothered to rise at all that morning. The long winter term had already dragged on forever and we weren't even halfway through yet. I could hardly remember the summer holidays, and those blue skies were now hidden behind a thick layer of cloud that rolled over the mountaintops.

No matter how far back I stood in the bus shelter, it was impossible to avoid getting wet. When the bus arrived, its front wheel hit a large puddle, ensuring that any part of me that had been dry was now wet.

"Ready, Eddie?" said the driver. "Then jump on board and hold on steady, Eddie."

Bill, the bus driver, made the same journey every day along the winding road that connected the towns, villages,

and clusters of houses in the valley. He had rhyming greet-
ings for all the pupils. They were set on the first day he
picked you up and remained unchanged until the last day
he dropped you off.

I found my usual seat next to Angus.

"Morning," he said. "Anything amazing to report?"

"Funny you should ask," I replied. "Last night I caught
a jet to Hawaii. First class, of course. I joined a circus,
learned to juggle fire, ate the world's biggest hamburger,
and wrestled a live bear."

"Better than a dead one."

"A dead one would have been easier."

Angus smiled. "I've been busy finalizing the project,"
he said.

"Finalizing the project," I repeated. He made it sound
like we were working on some kind of secret government
mission rather than climbing trees.

"That's right," he said, ignoring my sarcasm. "You and I
are going to attempt the Ten Tops Challenge—something
never attempted before."

"Maybe that's because it's pointless."

"Pointless? Was it pointless to climb Everest? Was it
pointless to reach the North Pole or land on the moon?
No. It needed to be done, as does this. Ten trees, seven
days, us two. This, my soggy friend, is the stuff of dreams."

"Who dreams about climbing trees?" I said, knowing

the answer full well. Angus dreamed about climbing trees. He had spent weeks preparing for this midterm break, identifying the ten tallest trees in the valley and setting us the challenge of climbing every one. I never understood his obsession, which seemed like one you'd have when you were eight, not fifteen. But, since I could never think of anything better to do, I went with him, although I was more cautious and often insisted we stop and go back down.

The valley was such a boring place that you had to go out of your way to find anything even remotely thrilling to do, which might also have explained Bill's driving. He rarely slowed down for corners, but even he had to lift his foot off the accelerator when it came to one sharp turn. We all called it Death Drop Point because, even though it was more of a big slope than a sudden drop, there was a story about a woman who lost control of her car once and drove over the edge.

Her name was Melody Dane.

She was my mother.

Angus drew a face in the condensation with his index finger. Two large droplets ran down from the lips and made it look like a vampire. Bill slammed on the brakes and stopped the bus, sending us into the seats in front.

"One of these days he'll kill someone," said Angus.

"I wonder why we're stopping here," I said.

"We must have a newbie." Angus wiped away the vampire face. "Funny day to start school, the Thursday before the midterm break."

A girl stepped onto the bus. Her coat hood hid her face, but her red, curly hair poked out the sides.

"Wellcome Valley School?" said Bill.

"Yes," she replied.

"That's lucky, because it's the only place we go." Bill looked as though he was hoping for some acknowledgment of what he considered a joke, but none came. "What's your name, then?"

"Scarlett White."

It was a credit to Bill's rhyme-making abilities that he barely needed time to think about it. "All right, Miss White, take a seat and hold on tight."

The girl pushed her hood back, allowing her hair to drop onto her shoulders and turning my brain to mush. This girl with her yellow raincoat, red hair, and green-blue eyes was the single most colorful thing I had ever seen in our gray valley. I must have been staring, because she threw me a funny look before sitting in the seat in front of us.

Angus leaned forward and said, "That's set in stone now."

"What?" The girl turned to look at him between the seats.

"Bill's rhyme. Every time you get on the bus, you'll hear

that. Until the end of time. He's got a memory like an elephant."

"And the driving skills of one too," replied the girl as the bus lurched sharply around a corner.

Angus elbowed me, but I was still trying to remember how to talk. The girl turned back around and Angus nudged me again.

"Where did *you* come from?" I blurted out.

It came out wrong. It sounded like I was accusing her of having jumped out from a hiding spot. I put the emphasis on *you* when it should have been on any other word in what had been a stupid question in the first place.

The girl didn't seem to notice and replied, "I just moved here."

"Then welcome to Wellcome Valley," said Angus. "Wherever you've come from, it won't compare to the thrills and spills that await you here. We've got it all, haven't we, Eddie?"

I smiled stupidly.

Angus continued. "Oh yes, we've got rain, clouds, sheep, hills, trees. I could go on but, well . . . that's it, isn't it, Eddie?" Angus chuckled. "In fact, sometimes we get worried we're going to burst with excitement, don't we, Eddie?"

Why did every single one of Angus's statements have to end with a question directed at me? Couldn't he see I had lost the ability to speak?

I was grateful when the girl responded. "It seems okay here to me."

Angus snorted. "Okay? You've arrived in literally the dullest place on the planet and you think it seems okay. Just you wait, eh, Eddie?"

CHAPTER 3

THE VALUE OF COMMUNITY

A COUPLE OF MONTHS INTO LIPHOOK'S FIRST JOB ON the Wellcome Valley police force, Sergeant Copeland had asked her to go and talk to a hall full of schoolchildren about the value of community.

She had never been comfortable speaking to a crowd, so she watched with dread as the children filed into the hall. Back then, Liphook was a young, eager, and ambitious police constable, and Wellcome Valley was the last place she wanted to be. One day she hoped to become a detective and solve real crimes, just like her fictional heroes who had inspired her to join the force—but first she had to get through this school assembly.

"How long have you been teaching at the school?" she asked Mrs. Lewis, the deputy head.

"Fifteen years," she replied, twitching her head and

scowling at children in that way Liphook remembered teachers doing when she was at school.

"Fifteen years," repeated Liphook, hoping the horror in her voice wasn't too obvious.

"Yes, I was a student at the school too. Wellcome Valley is one of those places that seeps into your pores."

A shiver ran down PC Liphook's back at the thought of this dull place infecting her blood. Personally, she intended to get out as soon as possible.

Once the hall was full, Mrs. Lewis gave a short introduction, warning the children to listen, and then Liphook began.

"*Community*," she said. "Who can tell me what that word means?"

Not a single hand went up.

"Come on," said Mrs. Lewis with an exasperated sigh.

Three kids raised their hands. Liphook pointed at them, one at a time, and they gave their answers.

"Looking out for each other."

"Being selfless."

"Sticking to the rules."

Liphook nodded, then looked down at her cards and talked nervously about the importance of acting responsibly, being good citizens, and about the role of the police. Unfortunately, her planned speech was considerably shorter than the time allotted, and when she glanced at her watch, she was dismayed that she had barely filled ten minutes and had run out of things to say.

"Maybe we should pause here for some questions," she said, praying that someone had a question.

Looking out into the hall, she saw that most of her audience appeared as bored as she was. One hand went up.

"Yes?" said Liphook. "What's your question?"

"Have you ever shot anyone?" asked the pupil.

"No. Armed police are a special division. Police officers such as myself do not carry guns." She tried not to sound as disappointed as the boy looked.

Another hand. "Have you ever been shot?"

"No," she said.

Mrs. Lewis was back on her feet. "Does anyone have a question not about shooting?"

A young boy in the front row asked, "Have you ever shot a gun at all?"

"That's still about shooting," warned Mrs. Lewis.

PC Liphook would have been happy talking about guns and shooting for the rest of the session, but Mrs. Lewis seemed keen to move things on. "I've got a question, actually," she said. "Tell me, Officer Liphook, is it true that Wellcome Valley has the lowest crime rate in the country?"

"I think there's an island in Scotland with lower figures, but that's because it's populated mostly by sheep," replied Liphook.

"Doesn't that make your job really boring?" asked a boy three rows back.

"Angus Sandling, how many times do I have to say 'Hands up' if you have a question? Besides, I am sure Officer Liphook has quite enough to occupy her here."

"That's right," lied Liphook. "Besides, police work can cover all kinds of things. It isn't like it's made to look on TV."

"You mean interesting?" said Angus, making the whole hall laugh and causing Liphook's cheeks to redden. "Don't you wish there would be a murder or something?"

"Do I have to send you out, Angus?" demanded Mrs. Lewis before turning to Liphook. "I'm very sorry about this."

"It's quite all right," said Liphook. "I'd like to answer that one, if it's all right with you."

"Oh, really? Very well." Mrs. Lewis sat down.

"Who likes to watch detective shows?" asked Liphook, finally on a subject she could talk about.

Almost half the pupils put their hands up.

"Me too," said Liphook. "On TV, I can't get enough murder."

The laughter boosted Liphook's confidence.

"On TV, I love seeing bad people doing bad things. It's exciting and fun to watch. Can anyone tell me why?"

"Because someone gets killed," said a girl at the back.

"Yes, but people get killed by things other than murder," she said. "Car crashes, diseases, old age. Why don't we sit down and watch shows about those things? I'll tell you why. Because murder involves someone removing something unique: another person's life. There's no going back from that. It's not something that can be fixed or replaced. It's an irreversible crime. Kill someone and you have changed your life and the world forever. Not for the better, but for the worse."

There was silence in the hall. Liphook wondered why she had just given a speech about murder to a bunch of schoolkids. Considering how inappropriate this was, it was interesting to note that she had their attention more totally than at any other point during the talk. Even the teachers along the side of the hall who had been marking papers had stopped to listen.

"Well, I'm sure you all found that very informative," said Mrs. Lewis. "I know I've learned a lot about how we can make our community a better place. Let's show our appreciation for Officer Liphook."

CHAPTER 4

EMBRACING THE CHAOS

I WASN'T THE ONLY ONE IN CLASS WHO THOUGHT Scarlett worthy of attention. At lunchtime, I sat with Angus, watching all the various groups of girls buzzing around, trying to recruit her.

"It's only because she's new," said Angus.

"I don't think it's just that," I replied.

"'Course it is. Take these meatballs." He held one up on his fork. "Now, I like these meatballs, but if one Thursday they had something different—I don't know, sausages, maybe—I'd go for them because it'd be something different."

"You're wrong," I said. "It's because she clearly doesn't care about any of this. Look at her. She would happily sit there on her own, and they all know that. That's why they're all interested in her."

Scarlett glanced up from her food and caught my eye. I looked away.

"So, you're saying that this meatball only seems boring because it wants to be eaten," said Angus.

I laughed. "Exactly. What you need is a meatball that's not bothered about being eaten. That would be an amazing meatball."

Scarlett's popularity meant that by the time we were sitting down for English, the last lesson of the day, I had failed to add to the five words I had blurted at her on the bus. And now she was sitting on the opposite side of the room.

Mr. Cornish, who taught English, was different from the other teachers. While they all stood at the front during lessons, going on and on, Cornish moved around the room, engaged in a kind of strange dance to the different threads of conversation as they shot off in all directions. *Embracing the chaos* was how he put it. He believed that all ideas were worth expressing, which made him extremely easy to distract. He also had this funny idea about not allowing hands-up in class, instead plucking answers from whomever he chose. His classes were nerve-racking, but it did keep you on your toes.

Sometimes he gave me a lift home because he lived in the same direction. He liked to talk, whether it was about the environment or politics or personal things, like how I felt about growing up without a mother or father.

"Monsters," said Cornish once we had settled down. "I want us to name as many monsters as we can, comrades."

He always called us that. When we asked why, he said it meant *friend* and was as good a word as any. On his first day he had asked us to call him Patrick, but it felt weird so most of us stuck with *sir* or *Comrade Cornish* or just *Cornish*.

"Er . . . vampires?"

"Dragons."

"Werewolves."

Answers came from various parts of the room.

"Yes, shout them out. Let's fill the board." Cornish was embracing the chaos, trying to write down the names as fast as we could yell them.

"How about you, Scarlett?" he said once the obvious ones had been noted. "Can you add anything?"

All that day, the other teachers had needed to double-check the name of the new girl, but Cornish had obviously taken the time to learn it.

"Mankind," she replied.

Cornish tossed the marker pen in the air, spun around, clicked his fingers, and caught it. "Very good," he said. "I'd prefer we use the term *humankind*, but you're right; humans are the deadliest monsters of all."

"How d'you work that out?" asked a boy called Tom.

"Humans are responsible for creating all these other monsters." Cornish tapped the pen on the board.

"Humans didn't create dinosaurs," said Angus, who had suggested a T. rex as his monster.

"No, but we attached the label to it," said Mr. Cornish. "*Tyrannosaurus rex* was no different from any other species. It was born, grew up, ate a lot, pooped a lot, and died, just like we all do. Then we came along, dug up its bones, gave it a scary name, and turned it into a monster. In films, they're always attacking humans, but if there had been an evolutionary overlap, I'll bet you anything we would pose a much greater threat to them. We humans are more destructive and terrifying than any made-up monster. Which brings us to the book we'll be looking at over the next few weeks."

On his desk was a pile of books, which Cornish randomly distributed among the class. The one that landed in front of me had a picture of a bearded man sitting at a desk. It looked like an old painting. The man's skin had a yellowy glow from the candlelight, and he was holding a big jar of liquid. On the front was the title of the book: *Frankenstein.*

"Why are these books all different? Mine's falling apart," complained a girl behind me.

"Don't panic, comrades, they all have the same words on the inside," said Cornish.

"But we all know this story," said Angus. "Man makes monster."

"You mean you know what happens. That isn't the same

as knowing the story," said Cornish. "And, as you can see, I've managed to beg, borrow, and steal enough copies for you each to have one, but I will want the books back, so please treat them with respect." He snatched a copy from someone who had been bending back its spine. "So, can anyone tell me this book's alternative title?"

"*The Modern Prometheus*," said Scarlett.

"Very good, Comrade White," said Cornish, clearly impressed. "And do you know who Prometheus was?"

"He was an ancient Greek myth, who created man from clay and stole fire from the gods to give to humankind."

"Perfect. You see, comrades, ever since we crawled out of the primordial sludge, humans have created imaginary monsters. From Grendel to Godzilla, we have always invented things that terrify us, but what could be more terrifying than climate change or the destruction of the rainforests? What is more nightmarish than a nuclear fallout zone? Humans, with our endless desire to push back boundaries, are the greatest monsters of all. Which is precisely what Mary Shelley is trying to tell us in this, a book written when she was only a few years older than you. Now, let's see how she begins her masterpiece, shall we?"

CHAPTER 5

SOMETHING STRANGE

CORNISH GRABBED ME AS I WAS WALKING OUT OF CLASS. "I'm going straight off tonight, Eddie, if you want a lift home," he said.

"Thanks," I replied.

"How about you, Angus?" he asked.

"I'm getting picked up by the noise-mobile," Angus replied.

"Just you and me, then, Eddie," said Cornish. "I'll see you by the car once I'm done here."

I followed Angus into the corridor, having lost Scarlett in the throng.

"I thought you'd want to take the love bus home," said Angus.

"Shut up."

"Come on, you've been staring at her all day."

"It's not like that," I protested, trying to hide my embarrassment. "It's just that I think I recognize her from some-where."

"You mean from your dreams?" said Angus with a wide grin.

"No. From I'm not sure when." As I said this, I found myself wondering if there was some truth to my lie. Had I met Scarlett before? There was something familiar about her. When I first heard her voice, I realized it was how I had expected her to sound. But that couldn't be possible. That would mean I had forgotten her.

Angus and I stepped out into the drizzly car park, and I spotted her getting on the bus.

"Why do you think she's here?" asked Angus.

"What d'you mean?"

"Who moves to Wellcome Valley in the middle of term? Who starts school on a Thursday?"

"Last call for anywhere but here," yelled Bill.

"Never gets old," I said, watching the bus doors close.

Outside the gates, a car flashed its headlights. "I'd offer you a lift," said Angus, "only, with the terrible twins and the devil's spawn, it's lucky I can still get in myself. I've told my mum that's enough now. No more kids."

One of Angus's brothers opened the door, allowing the din from within to escape. Angus's mum was shouting at the twins while their baby brother screamed his head off, presumably so that he didn't feel left out.

"I'll see you tomorrow for more of the same," said Angus.

Once he had gone, there was nothing to distract me from the cold, so I was relieved to see Cornish leaving the school building. He was walking extremely quickly and I had to jog to get to his car at the same time. He stopped and looked at me. In the dim lighting of the car park, it was hard to read his expression, but it seemed as if he didn't recognize me.

"Are you all right, sir?" I asked.

"Eddie Dane?" He said it like he was plucking my name from the depths of his memory. He looked at the car keys in his hand, then back to me. "What do you want?" he asked.

"You offered me a lift," I replied, beginning to wonder if I had misunderstood.

"Did I? Yes, of course I did. Sorry, Eddie. Lots on my mind today."

He unlocked the car and we both got in. He looked at the dashboard, patted the steering wheel as though checking it wasn't a mirage, and started the engine. It revved louder than usual, and it took him a moment to find reverse.

"So, Eddie. Eddie Dane. How are you? How's your mother?" he asked.

"My mother, sir? She's . . . well, you know, still dead."

The indicator ticked as loudly as the clock in my grandma's living room. I had discussed my mother's death with Cornish a couple of weeks ago. He wanted to know how

I felt about it. I said it was ancient history. He said it was okay to feel sad about things that had happened a long time ago. I told him that when I was five or six years old, I would get so upset about it that I would hold my breath until I passed out. I said I didn't feel like that anymore. He asked how I did feel. I replied that I felt empty.

How could he have forgotten all that? "Dead?" he said.

"The last time I checked," I replied.

"Who killed her?"

"Who? No one. She . . . she died in a car accident."

"Right, and your father?"

"Er, I never knew him. Are you all right, sir?" I said.

He stared at me for an unnerving amount of time considering that he was driving and should have been looking at the road. "Sorry, of course, I got mixed up," he said at last. "Long day. You know how it is. I meant to ask about your . . . er . . ."

"My grandma?" I helped him out. "Ruby's fine. Well, you know, up and down, as usual."

"Right." He switched on the radio, fumbling with the controls so that it blasted out loud static. The signal was never very good this low in the valley. He turned it down but made no effort to tune it in. Songs and spoken words fought to be heard above the spitting, hissing noise. Neither Cornish nor I spoke for the rest of the journey. We listened to the static until we reached my house. He would have gone straight past had I not pointed it out. He slammed on the brakes. The car screeched to a halt and I opened the door, eager to escape.

"Look, Eddie," he said, "I'm sorry about me. Like I say, I've got a lot on my mind right now."

"It's okay," I said. "I'll see you tomorrow."

I slammed the door shut, then watched the red tail-lights of his car vanishing into the gloom.

CHAPTER 6

SOMETHING NOTHINGY

I FELT UNSETTLED AFTER THE JOURNEY WITH CORNISH, but the quiet burbling of a quiz show from the dimly lit living room indicated I had more pressing problems. Ruby was having one of her down days.

My grandma's life was divided into normal days, down days, and up days. On a normal day, she would go to the shops, cook dinner, and ask me about school, but these were getting increasingly rare. Given the choice, she preferred up days, when she had the energy to paint and create. On the down days, she could barely lift herself off the sofa to fetch a glass of water, but at least I didn't have to spend the evening cleaning paint off everything.

The sight of Ruby sprawled on the sofa with the curtains drawn, lit only by the flickering images of the TV, confirmed my suspicion.

"What are you watching?" I asked.

She looked up. "Something nothingy," she replied.

"How are you feeling?"

"The same."

"I'll make tea tonight, Grandma," I said, trying to remain upbeat. "You okay with pasta, Grandma?"

She nodded. The use of the banned G-word was intended to get a reaction, but she didn't even notice. I began to clear the coffee table of mugs and plates when something pricked my finger.

"Ow." I pulled it away and saw a droplet of blood.

"There's broken glass," said Ruby.

I switched on the main light.

"Too bright." She shrank back like a vampire in sunlight.

There was smashed glass all over the table from a broken picture frame. I swallowed my anger, checked that the photograph was intact, and went to find a dustpan and broom. In the kitchen, I noticed that the gas stove had been left on. I switched off the flickering blue flame and went back into the living room to clean up the mess. Once I had swept up all the bits of glass, I carried the frame to the kitchen, carefully removed the picture, and threw the rest in the bin with the glass.

It was typical down day stuff, but I was annoyed because it was the only picture I had of my mother. In the photograph, Melody was standing in front of an old green door. She was wearing dungarees and holding a hand up to shield her eyes from the glare of the sun. It was overexposed, so the top half of her face was too dark while the rest looked like a ghost. I had often wondered about what lay behind that green door and why my mother posed in front of it. Ruby said she didn't know where it was taken. From the pregnant swell of my mother's stomach, I had worked out it must have been a few months before I was born.

"Sorry," said Ruby, having finally hoisted herself off the sofa. "I had one of my moments."

"It's the only photo I've got," I said.

"I know. I'm sorry. Though, you know, Eddie, photos only show you what things look like on the outside," said Ruby. "It's more important to understand what's on the inside."

"She was my mother," I said. "I'd like to remember what she looked like on the outside."

In the living room, dramatic music came on the television as a quiz show contestant reached the final round.

"Don't idolize Melody," said Ruby.

"There's not much chance of that with you around to remind me what a terrible mother she was." I felt bad as soon as I said it. Not because it was unfair but because Ruby was unable to defend herself on down days.

"Life isn't a perfect thing," she said. "When your mother drove off that road, we both got lumbered, didn't we? I wasn't an award-winning mother the first time around, but Melody's death made prisoners of us both."

"We're all right, Ruby," I said, not wanting to send her spiraling any deeper into self-pity.

"You're a good lad, Eddie." Her voice quavered. Although it was her who had almost destroyed the only picture I had of my mother, it was now up to me to make her feel better. That's just how it was on down days. "I know ours is not much of a life," she said. "Maybe we'll do better next time, eh, lad?"

"I'll go and cook," I said.

"Thank you."

Before beginning the hunt for something edible in the kitchen, I carried the photograph to my bedroom. I slipped it inside my copy of *Frankenstein* and placed the book next to my bedside clock. It was my own fault for framing it and leaving it downstairs on the mantelpiece, but I had thought it might be nice to have some evidence of the missing member of our family. Angus's house was full of pictures of him and his brothers. There was an entire wall in the kitchen with photographs of them all at various ages and stages of their lives, including embarrassing ones of him naked as a baby. I loved that wall because it was full of memories. My life with Ruby wasn't like that. In our family, memories were something better kept hidden.

CHAPTER 7

CORNISHSTEIN

IT WAS RAINING EVEN HARDER ON FRIDAY MORNING. I stood at the bus stop working on a list of possible things to say to Scarlett, but I wasn't happy with any of them. When the bus arrived, I tried and failed to avoid the puddle splash before getting on.

"Ready, Eddie? Then jump on board and hold on steady, Eddie."

I found my usual seat next to Angus and filled him in on my strange journey home with Cornish.

"Maybe he's got amnesia," suggested Angus. "I saw this thing on TV about it once. It had this guy who woke up one day and forgot who his wife was. Mind you, when you saw the wife, you did wonder whether he was only pretending."

"I don't think Cornish had forgotten who I was," I said. "He remembered my name."

"But he forgot that he was giving you a lift home?"

"And about Melody."

"Are you sure you had told him?"

"Yes," I said. "It came up after that discussion we had in class about orphans a few weeks back. He was worried he had upset me."

"Maybe he's having a breakdown. I've never really understood what that means, though. Is it like when a car breaks down and you just need new bits?"

"Don't ask me. I don't think Ruby's ever worked well enough to break down."

The bus screeched to a halt.

"All right, Miss White, take a seat and hold on tight," yelled Bill.

I felt stupidly excited when Scarlett sat in the seat in front of us again, because it meant that this was now her seat of choice. There would be lots of opportunities to talk to her, which was handy because, yet again, I was dumbstruck by her presence, meaning that it was up to Angus to speak.

"How was your first day in the center of the universe?" he asked.

She swiveled around in her seat, gripping the side as Bill took a corner at the speed of a race-car driver with a death wish. "Why do you call it that?" she said.

"Oh, you know, because it's so exciting around here, isn't it, Eddie?" replied Angus.

"Thrilling," I said, bringing my total number of words in Scarlett's presence to six. Six! A baby could make better small talk than this. I needed to pull something good out of the bag if I was going to hold her attention.

"How do you know all that stuff about *Frankenstein?*" I asked. It was supposed to sound casual and offhand. It was supposed to sound interested but not desperate. It sounded like an interrogation.

"I've read it." She said it so dismissively that I wanted to die.

"*Frankenstein.*" Angus clicked his fingers. "That's it."

"What's he talking about?" asked Scarlett.

I was so distracted by the way she looked at me that I almost forgot to answer.

"No idea," I said eventually. Not a great reply, but nor was it wrist-slittingly awful.

"Eddie got a lift back with Comrade Cornish last night, but he'd lost his memory."

"What did he forget?" asked Scarlett.

"Just stuff," I said, not wanting to steer the conversation to my dead mother so soon. "I can't see what it's got to do with *Frankenstein,* though."

"So, imagine this: Cornish is taking this *Frankenstein* stuff too seriously." Angus spoke fast, getting carried away with the idea. "So, he's made his own monster, only unlike Frankie's big, groaning fella, this one looks exactly like Cornish."

"Cornishstein," I suggested. Seeing Scarlett's face, I wished I had stayed quiet.

"But the monster wouldn't have Cornish's memories, would it?" continued Angus.

"Was it like he had forgotten completely or like it was a distant memory?" asked Scarlett. Apparently she was taking the discussion seriously.

"Distant memory," I replied. "Or a bit like someone who had just woken up."

"Interesting."

"Just woken up!" exclaimed Angus. "Like Frankenstein's monster wakes up." He let out a long moaning sound and stuck his arms out.

"Have you even read the book?" asked Scarlett.

"No."

"I've started it," I said, pathetically hoping that would impress her. She didn't look impressed. "So, what do you think?"

"About *Frankenstein* or Mr. Cornish?" she replied.

In truth, I didn't really care which we were talking about so long as we were talking.

"About Mr. Cornish," I said.

"People go weird sometimes. It doesn't really mean anything. I'd forget about it if I were you."

CHAPTER 8

CONSEQUENCES OF ACTIONS

THERE WAS A SMALL CHEER WHEN AN INDOOR BREAK was declared because the alternative was standing outside in the cold drizzle for fifteen minutes. Scarlett was once again swamped by attention. I was trying not to be too obvious about watching her when Mr. Cornish entered and came over to where Angus and I were sitting.

"Eddie, can I have a word?"

"Hello, sir," said Angus, grinning. "Monstrous weather today."

"Yes," said Cornish dismissively. "In the corridor, please, Eddie."

I followed him out of the classroom to a spot in the corridor by a display of self-portraits painted in the style of Picasso. They had ears, eyes, and noses all over the place, and Angus and I had been giggling about them recently, imagining what it would be like if people really did look like that.

"I want to apologize for yesterday," he said. "When I saw you, I had just received a personal phone call so I was rather distracted."

"Is everything all right, sir?" I asked.

"Everything's fine. I imagine you're looking forward to midterm break next week."

"Yes, Angus has got this tree-climbing project," I said, trying to sound enthusiastic about it.

Cornish nodded, then fell silent for so long that I had to pretend to be interested in the pictures on the wall.

Eventually he said, "It's easier when you're young."

"What is, sir?"

"Everything, Eddie. When you're young, you have firmly held beliefs, but the older you get, the more you realize that life isn't black and white."

"Like penguins, sir?"

"What?"

"Penguins are black and white, sir. Although I don't think they're born like that, so I guess you're saying that life is the opposite of penguins, because they do become more black and white than they start off."

"Why are you talking about penguins, Eddie?"

"I'm not sure, sir. I saw this thing on television about them the other day."

"I'm trying to explain that what you do matters. I'm talking about the consequences of our actions."

"Is this about *Frankenstein*? Because I did start reading it last night, only I was really tired and I fell asleep, and I think I kind of dreamed a lot of what I thought I'd read. Is there a scene with a penguin, sir?"

Cornish ignored the question. "*Frankenstein*," he said vaguely. "Yes, *Frankenstein*."

There was still something peculiar about him, and I was extremely relieved when the bell rang. "I'd better go then, sir," I said. "I'll see you this afternoon."

"This afternoon?" he repeated.

"For English, sir. I've got you last lesson."

"Of course," he replied.

I walked as quickly as I could back to the classroom, where I found Angus.

"Well?" he asked.

"Definitely a monster," I said.

CHAPTER 9

THE MEANING OF ACCIDENTS

ANGUS PLAYED CHESS AT LUNCHTIME ON FRIDAYS, SO I was sitting on my own when Scarlett entered the dining hall. I didn't want her to think I was some sad, friendless loser, so I stared down at my chips, trying to ignore her, but even in a crowded dining hall it was impossible not to notice her as she made her way toward me.

"You don't mind if I sit here, do you?" she said.

I did my best to look surprised by her sudden appearance.

"It's a free country," I replied.

It was supposed to sound cool but it just sounded rude. The problem was that every time she looked directly at me with her green-blue eyes, it felt like someone was pumping huge clouds of confusion into my brain, making normal conversation impossible.

"I can sit somewhere else if you'd prefer," she said.

"No. Please. Don't." From the desperation in my voice, you might have thought she had just threatened to turn off my oxygen supply.

She sat down. "Where's Angus?"

"Angus?" Why was she talking about Angus? Was she interested in Angus? Was that what this was about? She liked Angus?

"Boy about your age, dark hair, sits on the bus next to you," she said.

"Oh, that Angus. Yes. Chess club." They weren't long sentences, but they were better than nothing.

"Funny. I didn't have Angus down as a chess player," she said.

"He's only in it for the biscuits."

Scarlett smiled, which was definitely a step in the right direction, but I knew I had to keep the chat light. I wanted to show her I could be funny. I racked my brain for a list of conversation topics. I was still sifting through the possibilities when she said, "So, I hear your mum died when you were little."

"Er . . ."

"Sorry. That probably wasn't very sensitive."

"No, it's fine. She died a long time ago. If I'm not over it now . . . You know." I was scrabbling for the right response.

"How did she die?" she asked.

"In a car crash," I replied. "Ruby says driving was never one of Melody's strong points. Ruby's my grandma."

"You refer to your mother as Melody?"

"It was her name. Apparently she hated it."

Scarlett nodded. "Where did it happen?"

Most people, when they hear about my mother's death, either are overly sympathetic or avoid the subject altogether. Scarlett was asking about it as casually as though it was a show on television she had missed.

"Death Drop Point," I said.

"I don't know where that is."

"It's down the valley road, just before your stop."

"So you go around it every day?"

"Every school day. Who told you she died, anyway?"

"One of those girls. I forget which one."

I glanced at a table of girls, all pretending they weren't watching us. This was big. My mother's death was not the sort of thing people just brought up, which meant that Scarlett must have asked about it.

"Why did you want to know about it?" I asked.

"I'm interested in that sort of thing," she said.

"In death?"

"In accidents."

"You're interested in accidents?"

"Yes. Did you know that the word *accident* didn't always mean something bad? A few hundred years ago, it could be used for any event, good or bad. Over the years, though, it changed. Why did it change?"

"Because most things worth talking about are bad?" I suggested.

"Exactly."

"How do you know all this stuff?"

"I told you. It's something I'm interested in. So, what do you know about the accident your mother was involved in?" she asked. "I mean, if you don't mind talking about it."

If it meant she was looking at me, I didn't mind talking about anything. "Melody was upset when she got into the car because she'd been arguing with Ruby. My grandma still hates leaving an argument unsettled because of it."

"Do you know what they were arguing about?"

"No, but they didn't get on. Ruby says they were always arguing about something. She puts it down to her being artistic and Melody being more sciency."

Scarlett smiled to herself. "Sciency," she repeated, amused by the word. She picked up her fork to eat her salad.

I bit into a disappointingly cold chip, feeling weirdly aware of how much noise my mouth made when I ate. I tried to chew quietly, but the whole process of eating felt alien to me with Scarlett so close. In an attempt to distance Scarlett from the fact that I had forgotten how to eat, I swallowed the chip and asked, "So, where did you move from?"

"Look, Eddie, I'd rather not go into any of that, if you don't mind," she replied.

It struck me as odd that, having just listened to me go over the details of my mother's death, Scarlett was unwilling to even tell me something as basic as that.

"Is your family in one of those witness protection schemes or something?" I asked.

She grinned. "No, but I like that. I might use that in the future."

"Wherever you came from, I'll bet it was more exciting than Wellcome Valley. Round here, people think it's a big deal when there's a wall of drying paint to watch."

Scarlett put her knife down and placed her hand on top of mine. "It won't always be like this," she said softly.

A couple of girls at a nearby table noticed and whispered to the others. I pulled my hand away and instantly regretted it.

"Sorry," said Scarlett. "I don't mean to make you feel uncomfortable."

"I'm not. You don't. It's fine. It's just . . ."

I wished I had left my hand there, but the moment had passed. I selected another chip, hoping it would be warmer than the last one.

CHAPTER 10

A CHOICE OF BISCUITS

THE DAY AFTER THE TALK AT THE SCHOOL, LIPHOOK was sitting opposite Sergeant Copeland in his office while he noisily slurped from his cup of tea. He put it down and a droplet of milky brown liquid ran down the side, staining Liphook's application for a transfer.

"I wouldn't want you to rush into any decisions you might regret." Sergeant Copeland knitted his fingers together, then rested his hands on his round belly. "I know it's not exactly all car chases and stakeouts, but this kind of bread-and-butter community policing is very important. Now, which will it be? Digestive or Bourbon?"

"I don't want either, sir," said Liphook.

Sergeant Copeland was a nice man, and Liphook felt bad bringing up her request for a transfer again. Realizing that her refusal sounded overly curt, she added, "Thank you, though, sir. It's very kind of you."

"Come now, Liphook. You can't really have a cup of tea without a biscuit, can you?"

Deciding that the path of least resistance was easiest, Liphook took a digestive. She dunked it in the tea, but half of it broke off and dropped into the cup.

"I know what it's like to be hungry, you know," said Sergeant Copeland. "I mean, for more than biscuits." He chuckled, spraying Liphook with a small shower of crumbs.

"Yes, sir," she replied, watching him take two more Bourbons and shove them into his mouth.

"You're hungry for adventure and excitement, but you need to remember that you have a long career ahead of you. There will be plenty of opportunity for that sort of thing. Please, give it a few more months here. These hills, this valley, these people . . . you'll find they become a part of you."

"I need to get out, sir. I'm sorry," said Liphook.

"And go where?"

"Anywhere." Liphook instantly regretted saying it. She knew that Sergeant Copeland took personal exception to her desire to leave, but she desperately wanted to get some real policing experience under her belt. Seeing Sergeant Copeland's large, watery eyes fill with sadness, she did the only thing she could think of to cheer him up. She took another biscuit.

Sergeant Copeland smiled. "Ah, the digestive. A very underrated biscuit. Unfairly overshadowed by its flash-ier, more chocolaty cousins but every bit as important. A dependable, honest biscuit. I thought a thrill seeker like yourself would prefer the Bourbon."

"In all honesty, sir, I've always found Bourbons extremely disappointing." Sergeant Copeland let out a small gasp, but Liphook couldn't stop herself.

"It pretends to be chocolate, sir, but it's not. It's a chocolate-flavored, chocolate-colored biscuit. If you're going to eat a chocolate biscuit, then eat one. Or better still, have a chocolate bar, but don't settle for this." She picked up a Bourbon and waved it angrily at him. "This is a waste of everyone's time. This can only fail, both as chocolate and as a biscuit."

Sergeant Copeland leaned forward and plucked the Bourbon from her hand, then pointedly dunked it in his tea and gobbled it down. "Ah. This is nice, isn't it? Sitting here, talking about biscuits."

Liphook sighed. "Yes, it's just not exactly why I joined the force."

"Tell me, why *did* you join the force?"

"To make a difference, sir. I want to help people."

"You do help people. Only the other day, Mrs. Hitchcock told me how you gave her a lift home from the supermarket and helped her with her shopping."

"But I could be saving lives."

"I rather think that Mrs. Hitchcock trying to get all that shopping home on her own would have killed a woman of her age. Don't undervalue what we do, Liphook. You might not be chasing gun-toting gangsters every day but, little by little, we are making a difference. You are keeping Wellcome Valley safe. I know that you think this isn't the real world, but it's no less real than one of these big cities you're eager to work in."

"I'm not saying that what we do isn't important," protested Liphook. "It's about me. I need to spread my wings."

Sergeant Copeland picked up the tea-stained application form. "I'll tell you what, why don't we give it one month? If you haven't changed your mind after that, I'll give you a first-class recommendation for a transfer anywhere you want, and I'll try to drum up as much serious crime as I can during that time to keep you happy. Maybe I'll even commit a few crimes and you could chase after me."

"That's very kind of you, sir," said Liphook.

"Don't look so downhearted," said Sergeant Copeland. "As it happens, I do have something that might tickle your fancy."

He picked up a piece of paper from his desk and handed it to Liphook. On it was a photograph of a smiling girl with short blond hair and green-blue eyes.

"A missing person, sir?"

"Yes. Her name is Lauren Bliss. She vanished from her London home the day before yesterday. Apparently no problems at home or school. Generally well behaved, works hard at her studies, but two days ago she upped and vanished. Hasn't been seen since."

Liphook looked at the picture. "Any reason she would come here? We're a long way from London."

"Her parents don't know where she's gone, but apparently they came here on holiday last summer. They think she may have made a friend here. I'm afraid it's all a bit vague, but you never know."

"It does sound like a bit of a stretch."

"Ah, but as they say, if there are biscuits in the tin, there's always the possibility of finding a chocolate one."

"I'm sorry, sir. I don't follow."

"Where there's possibility there is also hope, Liphook."

CHAPTER 11

MELANCHOLY AND DESPAIRING

I DIDN'T GET A CHANCE TO TALK TO SCARLETT AGAIN that afternoon. By the time we were sitting down for English, we had been stuck inside all day again, so no one was in the mood to listen to Cornish going on about *Frankenstein.*

"Mary Shelley begins her story not at the beginning, but at the end," he said. "We are introduced to Frankenstein not as an innocent man, but as a man plagued by what he has done. He is . . ." Mr. Cornish looked down at the page and read, "*Melancholy and despairing.*" He repeated the words. "*Melancholy and despairing.* Why?" He pointed at a girl called Hannah, who looked startled by his question.

"Because he's made a monster?" she suggested.

"Not good enough," stated Cornish. "It's because he is living with the consequences of his actions. Victor Frankenstein is an enlightened man, an intelligent man, a scholar. He has no excuse of ignorance. Therefore he is forced to face the true horror of the terrible thing he has done. He is a prisoner of his own self-judgment."

"I think it would be pretty cool to make a monster," said Angus.

"Have you read the book yet, Angus?" snapped Cornish.

"No, but—"

"I suggest you contain your opinions until you've read the actual words." Cornish slammed his book down on Angus's table. "Mary Shelley's masterpiece is a story that has permeated our world. It is impossible to come to it without some preconception of what it's going to be about, but even a book that has been written can change. What do I mean by that? Anyone?"

"You mean when the author redrafts it?" said someone at the back.

"No. I'm talking about how it changes when we read it. Words come to life under our scrutiny. That spark which Frankenstein uses to bring his monster to life is there at the moment a reader connects with a book."

"The words don't change, though, do they?" said a boy by me.

"Not the words but the world around them. *That* changes, and it is up to you to ensure that it changes for the better, and not to accept your lot. I'm talking about fate. What do I mean by *fate*, Eddie?"

"Er, it's how things are going to happen in a certain way, no matter what you do," I said.

"And do you believe in fate, Eddie?"

"I suppose so," I said. "I mean, I think some things are meant to be." I realized I was staring at Scarlett and quickly looked away.

"So, you aren't in control of your life, Eddie?" Cornish asked. I was unsure why this was becoming all about me, and why he sounded so angry.

"Perhaps Eddie means that there is a natural and correct course of events," said Scarlett.

Cornish spun around on his heel and glared at her, then said, "Who decides this natural course of events? Who controls our fates? Those with money. Those with power. It's always the rich. The idea of fate is a tool of repression. The powerful have always preached to those with nothing that they must accept their lives and that there is nothing they can do about their situations. This is wrong. We should be the masters of our own stories."

"Are we still talking about *Frankenstein*?" asked Angus.

"Yes, we are still talking about *Frankenstein*."

"So, it's about fate, is it?" asked someone else.

"About fate? Come on, comrades, we're better than this. You can't reduce a book to one word. This is a book about love; that is a book about fate; this one is about kittens. Would you do that to a person? What are you about? Books are about every single word they contain."

We were used to Mr. Cornish getting overexcited, but he did seem angrier than usual today. "Next week, as well as wasting your lives with zombie-killing computer games and trivial television shows, I would like you to read this book yourselves."

A groan went up from the class. "The whole thing?" someone shouted.

"Yes, *read*. I realize this is a revolutionary concept, but perhaps that's what the world needs. Like it or not, you lot are going to inherit a world in which the progression of science will need to be questioned and challenged. And as you read these words, I want you to count how many times you find yourself hoping that Victor Frankenstein will do the right thing and not create the monster."

"But we already know he will," said Angus.

"And yet it is in our nature to empathize and hope that Victor Frankenstein changes course."

"I disagree," said Scarlett. "I think we want him to make the monster."

"Why would you want that?" demanded Cornish.

"Because it makes a good story," she replied, "and we know it's not real."

"The idea of scientists dabbling in things they should leave well alone is real enough," said Mr. Cornish.

"How about playing God?" asked Scarlett.

"We are all gods," hissed Cornish. "Anyone who creates, anyone who lives and breathes. Prometheus is the artist.

He's the creator. The question is not whether we should play God, but how we should do so responsibly."

When the final bell rang, the whole class walked out quieter than usual, wary of this new version of our English teacher sitting at his desk, clutching his copy of *Frankenstein*.

"What was that all about?" asked Angus once we were out of the room.

"Don't ask me," I replied. "You catching the bus?"

"No. Dad's coming to pick us up. We're going to see that new space film. I could ask if we could squeeze you in?"

"Sounds good, but Ruby will be expecting me."

"All right, suit yourself. Come around tomorrow and we'll begin the project."

"The project?" I replied.

"The Ten Tops Challenge. You and I on a mission of discovery, boldly going where no one has gone before. Reaching new heights—"

"Climbing trees," I interrupted.

"Climbing trees," repeated Angus.

CHAPTER 12

CONSPIRACY THEORIES

"ANOTHER THING THAT NEVER CHANGES HERE AT THE National Museum of Echo Technology is the recording made by Professor Maguire," said the man in the orange T-shirt, "in which he demonstrated how echo jumping works."

A screen showed a man in a white coat. "My name is David Maguire and this is a scientific demonstration," he began.

"Turn it off," said Liphook.

The nice young man waved his arm and the image vanished. "Of course, you've seen it before," he said apologetically. "Everyone has."

"It's not that," said Liphook. "It's just that before that message, before all this . . ." She gesticulated around her. "The world was simpler back then. Things made sense."

"Echo technology is certainly complicated, but if you'd

care to visit the explanation room, you'll find very clear displays about the time particle, version creation, and echo jumping."

"I'm not interested in any of that," said Liphook dismissively.

The young man looked momentarily confused by this. "Then why are you here?" he asked.

"To remember."

He smiled. "Of course, people visit for all sorts of reasons. We get a lot interested in the truth behind David Maguire's murder. Apparently there are now over two hundred different theories about who did it and why."

"I don't care about that either," said Liphook. "I know the truth."

From the young man's expression, Liphook could tell he had heard this before, but she couldn't be bothered to explain that she was different from all the other conspiracy theorists. She knew the truth, and it had turned out to be more outlandish than the most extraordinary theory.

Liphook realized the man had spoken. "I'm sorry?" she said. "What was that?"

"I was asking about your theory," he said.

"It's not a theory," she said. "At least, it's not my theory. I'm not even sure if it's our truth, but it was someone's truth. I don't suppose this makes much sense to you, does it?"

The man kindly avoided answering the question. "Personally, I don't think we'll ever know the truth, but did you really come here when Maguire still lived here?"

"Only once."

"When?"

"I came the day he died."

13

PLAUSIBLE LIES

I HAD NEVER THOUGHT THE BUS SEATS TOO SMALL before, but with Scarlett sitting next to me, I had no idea what to do with my arms. The whole setup felt ridiculously awkward. As a last resort, I gripped my elbows to avoid any unnecessary contact.

"Are you cold?" asked Scarlett.

"No. I'm fine."

"Only, you look like you're cold."

I placed my hands on my knees instead and the bus went lurching forward like a hiccuping camel, making it impossible for me to avoid banging into Scarlett. I had considered a number of conversation topics but decided to stick with the one that I knew she was interested in.

"You know how you asked all that stuff about the car accident?" I said.

"Yes."

"It's funny, because that's what Cornish had forgotten."

"He thought Melody was alive?"

"Yes, which was odd because we talked about it only the other day."

"Why didn't he give you a lift home tonight?"

"I think he had a meeting. He doesn't always give me a lift."

"Where's his house?"

"Down in Lower Marsh, in this funny little row of houses they call No Town."

"No Town?"

"Yeah. Apparently someone had an idea of building a town there once, but they only got as far as that row before they ran out of money. Or the ground was too soft. Or something like that. Maybe it's not true."

I was babbling and, from the distracted look on Scarlett's face, I had lost her interest. I needed to get it back.

"That was weird in class, wasn't it?" I said.

"You tell me. You know him better than I do. Is he normally like that?"

"He often goes off on a rant, but no, all that stuff about fate and inheriting the world was a bit odd. Why do you want to know where he lives?"

"It's probably better if I don't answer that," she replied.

There was a sudden jolt as Bill sped over a pothole in the road.

"I don't get it. You're happy asking questions about my dead mother, but when I ask you even basic things about you, you won't answer." I had hoped this would sound jokey, but it came out more upset and annoyed.

"Yes, that must seem unfair," she agreed.

"I'll tell you what," I said, "what about if I guess why you're so secretive and you tell me if I get it right?"

The smallest of smiles spread across Scarlett's lips. "All right, but it has to be completely right."

I thought for a moment, then said, "Are you a kind of alien secret agent who thinks that Mr. Cornish has been possessed by an extraterrestrial life-form and you want to know where he lives so you can zap him with an antimatter gun that will send the alien back home?"

I loved the sound of Scarlett's laughter.

"Have you got any more like that?" she said.

"Loads. You're an undercover cop and you think Mr. Cornish has been hypnotized to kill the prime minister?"

"Why would someone hypnotize an English teacher to kill the prime minister?"

"Because they know about the big conference he's going to that the prime minister will also be at."

"Is there such a thing?" she asked.

"You tell me."

More laughter. "These are good but not close enough for me to tell you anything. To be honest, Eddie, I'd be in enough trouble if anyone knew you thought there was anything to know."

"In trouble with who?"

"The fact you're asking that means you know too much."

"But I don't know anything."

"Exactly."

"I've *got* it," I said.

"Is this going to be Angus's monster theory again?"

"No. In this one, you're the bad guy who has taken over Cornish's mind and you're using him to execute your evil plan."

"To kill the prime minister?"

"No, to blow up the school."

"Wow, I'm so evil."

"Is that one right, then?"

"No." She paused and I realized how close our lips were. I wondered what my breath was like. I kept my mouth shut, just in case.

"What I'm supposed to do now is feed you some plausible lie," she said quietly, "but I don't want to do that. I'd rather tell you the truth."

"Sounds good to me."

"The truth is I can't tell you anything."

"I'll take a plausible lie, then," I said.

I happily bagged another of Scarlett's smiles. This one was my favorite so far because it included her eyes. "All right," she said. "I'm going around tomorrow to ask him some questions about *Frankenstein*."

"Really?"

Scarlett sighed. "Eddie, the world is very complicated and you're very young."

"We're the same age," I protested.

"It's not worth getting interested in me. I'm not going to be here very long," she said.

"Maybe you'll like it here and stay," I said hopefully.

"It's not my decision."

"Would you stay if it was?" I was desperate for some signal that she felt the same way I did.

"Would I stay here in this valley?" She gazed out the window, staring directly into the eyes of her own reflection. "Would I stay here and catch the bus with you every day, Eddie Dane? Over time, would we become best friends? Then become . . ." Her voice trailed away and she left the sentence unfinished. "Would we make promises to each other, Eddie? One day, would I believe I knew you better than I know myself?"

"My question was simpler," I said.

She smiled.

"Well?" I asked. "Would you stay if you could?"

Her final smile was the saddest so far and contained

traces of pity and other things I didn't understand. "I probably would," she said.

The bus suddenly lurched to the right, and Scarlett's face swung even closer to mine. Bill slammed on the brakes.

"All right, Miss White. We're home. Good night," yelled Bill.

"See you around, Eddie Dane," she said.

14

A PICTURE
OF REGRET

THE UNLOCKED FRONT DOOR, THE STRONG SMELL OF paint, and the sound of scratchy jazz records meant Ruby was having an up day. Ruby's paintings were as messy and chaotic as the music that inspired her, and it was rarely just the canvases that got spattered.

As I stepped into the front room, I saw flecks of red, blue, yellow, and green across the wall, the carpet, and the sofa, even reaching as far as the grandfather clock and the television. In the middle of all this stood Ruby.

"What do you think?" she asked.

"It's great," I lied. "What is it?"

"Regret," she replied.

I had learned not to question this kind of thing. Instead I said, "Have you been to the shops?"

"No, but I think there are a couple of ready meals in the freezer."

"I thought we weren't eating ready meals anymore. I thought they were symbolic of something."

"The soul-crushing instant gratification of the modern world," said Ruby. "Yes, they are. But I've been working on this all day and haven't managed to make it out. It's just so hard to . . ." Apparently it was too hard to find the right word for what it was too hard to do. Ruby turned back to the canvas and I went into the kitchen. I noticed I had a smudge of green paint on my shirt. I took the shirt off and threw it into the washing machine.

"Striptease, is it?" said Ruby, following me in.

I showed her the paint.

"I'm sorry, love. Have you a clean one for tomorrow?"

"It's Saturday tomorrow," I replied, "and then midterm break."

"Is it? Is it? Any big plans?"

"Angus has a tree-climbing project."

"Sounds fascinating." Ruby opened the freezer and pulled out two boxes covered in ice. "What do you fancy? Tagliatelle or a roast meal? Actually, do you mind if I have the tagliatelle? I always think those roast meals taste a bit like the kind of thing you get given in an old folks' home, and I might be old, but I'm not ready for that quite yet."

"Is it about Melody?" I asked.

"The ready meal?"

"The painting. The regret. Is it about her?"

"Your mother is in there, of course."

"So, what's the regret?"

"It's complicated. It's not one thing. But your mother and I were very different people. I wish we had learned to accept our differences and worked harder on the things we had in common."

"What did you have in common?"

"We had you in common."

"Is the painting finished?" I asked.

"It's a picture of regret," said Ruby. "It can't be finished."

15

A BURIED BOOK

THAT NIGHT, I TRIED AND FAILED TO GET FURTHER through *Frankenstein*, but whether I was too distracted by Ruby's records or by the thought of Scarlett, I struggled to take in the words.

When I woke up on Saturday morning, the book was open on the pillow next to me. I picked it up and read the sentence at the top of the page:

> *I have described myself as always having been imbued with a fervent longing to penetrate the secrets of nature.*

I liked that expression, *a fervent longing*. My whole life, the only thing I had ever longed for was to have something to long for. There were no secrets I wanted to penetrate. I didn't have any obsessions. Angus had his trees, Ruby had painting, and Cornish had all that stuff about books, politics, and the environment. I envied them all their passions. I had never cared about anything until Scarlett got on that bus.

The house was freezing cold and the bathroom mirror steamed up in seconds when I turned on the shower. I drew a face like the one Angus had drawn on the bus window, but the drips came down in a different part of the mouth, and it looked more like an uneven rabbit than a vampire.

It was still raining when I headed out, so I put on my most waterproof coat.

I was supposed to be going to see Angus, but since Cornish's house was on my way, there was no harm in keeping an eye out for Scarlett. "*Hey, Scarlett,*" I would say. "*What a coincidence. I was just cycling past. How are you?*" Something like that. It was best not to rehearse it too much.

It was a steady downhill slope to Lower Marsh, so I stopped pedaling and freewheeled down. I kept my hand on the brake to keep my speed down. There were twelve houses in No Town, and I soon reached the end with no sign of Scarlett. I turned the bike in a figure eight, looking around, then pedaled back past the houses, slower still. I considered cycling up to where she got on the bus to look for her house, but that felt too much like stalking her. This was more a case of cycling up and down a road, trying to catch a glimpse of her. Completely different.

After the third pass, I parked my bike in an alleyway

between two of the houses and went around the back, where there was a big patch of wasteland with long grass and marshy ground. That was where I finally saw Scarlett. She was crouching behind a hedge around the back of Cornish's house. She was wearing her yellow coat with the hood pulled up. I walked over as casually as the swampy ground would allow.

"Hey, Scarlett," I said. "What a coincidence. I was just..."

She silenced me with a look. "Eddie, you shouldn't be here. This isn't anything you can know about."

"What isn't?"

"I can't tell you. Stay out of sight."

I ducked down next to her. "What are we doing?" I whispered.

"*We* aren't doing anything. I am watching Patrick Cornish's house."

I peeked through the hedge at his back garden.

"Why?"

"Just so you know, the best you'll get as an answer to that question is a plausible lie," she said.

"How do you know he's in?" I asked.

"The light is on, and Patrick Cornish isn't the sort of person to waste electricity, is he?"

"True. He's always going on about all that environmental stuff. Only the other day—"

Scarlett placed her finger against my lips to shut me up. She had cold hands, but I didn't care. Her finger lingered there, and I felt unsure about whether to move my face away or leave it. Would it be weird to kiss her finger? Yes, I decided. It would be a bit weird. I looked at her, but she was staring through the hedge. Cornish had stepped into his back garden. In one hand he held a transparent bag with a red exercise book inside, in the other a spade. He took three carefully measured steps into the garden and dropped the bag.

Scarlett moved her finger away but threw me a glance warning me not to speak. Cornish thrust his spade into the grass and began to dig a hole. When he stopped, he picked up the book in the bag, chucked it in, and quickly shoveled the soil back over it.

Once he had patted it down, he took another step back in the direction of the house and dug a second hole. Having reached a similar depth, he dropped his spade and knelt down, only to pull out of this hole what looked like the same book in the same bag. Mr. Cornish carried it back inside.

"What was that? What happened?" I asked.

"He buried a book, then dug it up," replied Scarlett simply.

"Why?"

"Perhaps he wanted to grow a book tree."

"But . . . but it moved," I said.

"Yes," agreed Scarlett.

"How is that possible?"

"It will make it easier if you don't ask questions that I'm not going to answer," stated Scarlett.

"How do I know if it's a question you won't answer?"

"Perhaps avoid all of them, just in case."

"Maybe Mr. Cornish is some kind of magician," I said, careful not to phrase it as a question.

"Maybe," replied Scarlett.

"Is he?"

"No, and that's still a question."

"So, you understand what's going on but you won't tell me. Is that it?"

"I understand some of what is going on, and I will tell you this: burying books is pretty old hat where I'm from, and the fact that he thought your mother was alive is interesting. But what I really need to know is what he wrote in that book."

When the kitchen light went off, Scarlett stood up and hurried across the marsh. She didn't wait for me, but nor was she surprised when I followed her.

This was far too interesting to give up.

CHAPTER 16

THE WORD *PROTOCOL*

GROWING UP IN WELLCOME VALLEY, YOU GOT USED TO inventing things to occupy your time, but Scarlett's project felt different from Angus's. She wasn't climbing trees to kill time. I could tell she had a job to do. We stood out of sight, watching Cornish drive away, and then she took out a small notepad and pen from an inside pocket and scribbled something in it.

"What are you writing?" I asked.

Scarlett didn't even bother responding this time. She flipped the book shut and returned it to her pocket.

"I've got it," I said. "You wrote down his license plate."

"Why would I do that when the book is in the house?" she responded.

"I give up, then."

"I wish you would. Look, in a minute I'm going to do

something inexplicable, and then I'm going to break the law."

"Cool."

"No, not cool, Eddie," she said, her temper surfacing in her eyes and her nostrils flaring. "I'm running out of ways to tell you to go away."

"Admit it, I'm growing on you," I said.

Her smile was short-lived. "I've got to get into that house to look at the book," she said.

"You're going to break into his house?"

"I wasn't planning on breaking anything."

"You remember that talk on Thursday? We do have police here."

"How do you know I don't work for the police?"

"Because you're too young."

Scarlett bit her lip and looked down. "Eddie, do you know what the word *protocol* means?"

"Yes," I said. "Of course. Protocol. I know what it means. Protocol. Er, protocol."

"You don't know, do you?"

"Not exactly."

"A protocol is like a rule. And there are protocols about what I can and can't tell you."

"Who made these rules?"

"I can't tell you. That's one of the protocols."

"So, just to get this straight, you can't tell me who's told you not to tell me all the things you can't tell me? Is that right?"

"Correct."

"How will you get into the house, then? Will you open the door with a credit card or something?"

"I don't know how to do that," said Scarlett, "and you watch too much TV. You need a key to get into a house." Scarlett checked the time on her watch. "Ah, here we go. Remember, no questions."

That far down in the valley, the roar of the approaching motorbike echoed off the hills and made it sound as though it was all around, coming from every direction at once. When it appeared around the corner, I saw its rider dressed in black leather with the helmet visor down. He stopped directly in front of us and pulled something from his pocket, which he handed to Scarlett. I looked up at his face, but all I saw was my own reflection.

"Thank you," said Scarlett.

The biker didn't speak, but I felt he was looking at me.

"I've got it under control," said Scarlett firmly. "You can go now."

The motorcyclist nodded and twisted the right handlebar to accelerate. He was gone as suddenly and noisily as he had arrived, and soon the sound of the engine blended into the hiss of the constant rainfall. When Scarlett held up the object that had been dropped into her hand, I saw that it was a key. She winked at me and made her way down the path.

"Is that a magic notepad, then? Anything you write down gets delivered?"

"If it helps you to think that, yes."

"So, if you wrote down *pizza,* that guy would come back with a pizza."

"It would be easier to order a pizza from the pizza place but, yes, in theory. Now, try to act natural."

"What could be more natural than a mysterious man on a motorbike delivering a key to someone's house, then us using it to go inside?" I followed her down the path and inside Mr. Cornish's house.

"I always wondered how my life of crime would start," I said.

"You're talking a lot because you're nervous," said Scarlett. "It's perfectly normal, but try not to."

"Why? Are you worried someone might hear?" I whispered.

"No. It's just a bit annoying," she replied.

"So, what now? Should we split up and search?"

"No need. The book's on the coffee table. He clearly doesn't expect anyone to be following him. That should make this easier."

She picked up the red exercise book. I edged nearer to look. Inside, Mr. Cornish had written in his usual scrawl:

Primary target already dead. Please advise.

Below this, another pen had written:

Continue with project. Terminate secondary target.

"Do you know what that means?" I asked.

"Yes. It means I have to go."

"Go where?"

"To the museum."

"What museum?" I asked. "There's no museum around here."

"Not yet, there isn't."

CHAPTER 17

CAT THEFT

DURING THE TRIAL, LIPHOOK HAD BEEN ASKED TO GIVE an exact account of how she had come to arrive on the scene the day David Maguire was killed. She had begun with the first call of the day, when an elderly lady by the name of Mrs. Spinks reported her car stolen from outside the corner shop.

Liphook parked her patrol car outside and walked into the shop, where Mrs. Spinks was in a state of mild hysteria. The shop owner was doing his best to comfort her, but he looked extremely relieved to hand over responsibility to a uniformed officer. Liphook quickly established the facts. Mrs. Spinks was seventy-eight years old and her car had been stolen. Not the crime of the century, but better than nothing.

"Where was the vehicle when it was taken?" Liphook

hoped she sounded calm, serious, and yet fully in control of the situation.

"There. Where you've parked now," exclaimed Mrs. Spinks, pointing out the window. "My poor darling. He could be anywhere."

"And where were you?"

"Inside the shop, you silly girl. Where else would I do my shopping? Are you sure you're a real police officer?"

"Very much so, Mrs. Spinks, but I do need to establish exactly what happened."

"I parked my car outside and came in to buy a bottle of the red top. Not the blue top. He doesn't like the blue top, and no one likes the green top really, do they? Well, supermodels, perhaps."

Liphook was having difficulty following her. "Are you talking about milk?"

"Yes, of course."

"You were buying milk for your car?"

"Don't be ridiculous. Why would I do that? The milk was for Rascal."

"Who's Rascal?" Liphook was getting confused.

"My cat. That's why you're here. Keep up, dear."

"I thought you reported a stolen car."

"He said you wouldn't care if I only told you about Rascal." She pointed to the shopkeeper. "Is that true? I've paid taxes all my life to keep you lot in jobs. Don't you care about cats?"

The shopkeeper smiled sympathetically and shrugged.

Liphook turned back to Mrs. Spinks. "So, you drove here to buy milk for your cat, and then what?"

"They took Rascal."

"From your house?"

"Why would they go to my house?"

"Mrs. Spinks, was your cat in the car?"

"Yes, he likes to sit in the backseat." A worried expression crossed the old lady's face. "I say, do you suppose it was professional cat thieves? Rascal's parents were both pedigreed, you know."

"I think it's more likely they wanted the car and didn't realize it had a cat in the back."

"How will he ever find his way home?" asked Mrs. Spinks. "He never goes very far. He'll be terrified."

"Mrs. Spinks, please try to stay calm. So, how long did you leave your car unattended?"

"Only a couple of minutes. How long do you think it takes to buy milk?"

"A couple of minutes is very fast for someone to break into a car, hot-wire it, and drive off."

"What does *hot-wire* mean?"

"It's how a car thief starts a car without a key."

Mrs. Spinks looked quizzically at Liphook. "Why wouldn't they use the key?"

Liphook looked up from her notepad. "How would they get the key?"

"It was in the car. I find that if I take it out, I can never find it again."

"Are you saying that you left the car outside the shop with the key in the ignition?"

"Of course. How else could the engine be running?"

"The engine was running?" exclaimed Liphook.

"Oh yes, Rascal likes the vibration. I suppose it's a bit like purring, isn't it? Poor Rascal, he'll be frightened out of his wits."

"I promise that we'll do everything we can to recover your car and your cat, but I will need your license plate number."

"Rascal doesn't have a license plate number."

"Of the car."

"I have no idea," said Mrs. Spinks dismissively.

"A description, then."

"Yes, of course. Dark tabby, a cross between a Maine coon and a Siamese. Very friendly but a little jealous sometimes. Likes fish but not the processed kind. I get it from the fishmongers."

Liphook jotted down the details. "And the car?"

"Oh, I see. It's red and it has a cat in the back."

18

A CAT CALLED RASCAL

SCARLETT UNLOCKED THE SMALL RED CAR PARKED outside Cornish's house and got in.

"You drive?" I said.

It was amazing. Each time I thought she couldn't do anything else to surprise me, she did something even more surprising.

"I really need you to go away now," she replied wearily.

There was something about the way she used the tips of her fingers to rub her eyes that seemed strangely familiar. I quickly got into the car before she had the chance to drive off without me. "You're not old enough to drive," I said.

"And you're not stupid enough to get into a stolen car," she replied.

"It's stolen?"

"Yes. Do you still want to come? This is your last chance to get out. I really don't have time to argue with you."

"Let's go, then."

"Eddie Dane, you are the stubbornest person I have ever met."

Weirdly, even though she shouted the words and banged the dashboard in frustration, I didn't really feel she was genuinely angry. She sounded amused, as though she was repeating an often-told joke between us. I liked it. She turned the key and started the engine with the confidence of someone who had been starting cars all her life.

"You were joking about it being stolen, weren't you?" I said.

"Which answer do you want?"

"The one that means you've borrowed your mum's car or something."

"Fine. Then I did that."

"That's not true, is it?"

"What do you think?"

"Did the car key get delivered by another one of your magic motorbike people?" I asked.

"Don't call him that, and no. It was in the ignition." The noise the car made when Scarlett put her foot down suggested it was unused to being driven at such speed. Everything rattled in a terrified protest against her driving.

"Did Bill teach you to drive?"

"Actually, I had a very good teacher," she replied, keeping her eyes on the road.

I gripped the side as she took another corner without slowing down.

"Aren't there protocols about this?" I asked.

"To be honest, there are protocols about more or less everything, but you've got to have a little bit of fun too, otherwise what's the point? I'm sorry, am I making you nervous?"

The truth was that Scarlett didn't need to break the speed limit in a stolen car to make me feel nervous, but it wasn't the kind of nervous that made me want to get away. It was the kind of nervous that made me want to stay forever.

"Do you remember me saying my mum died in a car crash?" I said. "I didn't mean that it was a family tradition or anything."

She laughed. "What do you know about your mother, Eddie?"

"Not much."

"I mean, what did she do? Did she have a job?"

"I don't think so. She was still at university when she had me. She dropped out, I think."

"Hold on," said Scarlett. "We've gone past the turning."

She slammed on the brakes and I felt my whole body jerk forward, then rock back. Scarlett looked over her shoulder and put the car into reverse along the road, then turned right onto a dirt track that cut through a field.

Since it had rained continually for the past three days, we didn't get far before the car began to skid and slide in the mud, unable to go any farther.

Scarlett switched off the ignition and undid her seat belt. "We'll have to walk," she said. "When you get out of the car, move quickly and close the door behind you straightaway."

"Why?"

"So you don't let the cat out."

"What cat?"

"That cat."

She pointed over her shoulder to where a terrified-looking cat was digging his claws into the backseat. I reached down and inspected the collar around his neck. The cat was quaking in fear. He hissed at me as I read his tag.

"He's called Rascal," I said, stroking his head.

"Well, let's keep Rascal in the car. It's bad enough stealing an old lady's car, but losing her cat would be awful."

CHAPTER 19

THE GREEN DOOR

SCARLETT WAS WALKING FAST AND I WAS DOING MY best to keep up, but I was also trying to avoid the really deep puddles, which involved a lot of hopping and jumping.

"Do you have to do that?" she asked.

"I'm trying not to get my socks wet," I replied. "So, is your life always like this?"

"These days it is, yes. Things are more complicated where I'm from."

"You mean that we're all simple here in the valley?"

"Things are simpler here, yes."

I made a big jump to the other side of the path to avoid an enormous muddy puddle, which Scarlett had just walked straight through.

"You look like a demented frog," she said.

"A demented frog?" I replied, but Scarlett didn't laugh.

We were approaching a cluster of trees at the edge of the field. I had never been to this spot before. It was the sort of place that tourists liked. The valley was full of holiday cottages for city folk to hire so they could ramble through nature and get away from the hustle and bustle of their normal lives—an idea that made no sense to me.

"Just over that ridge is a farmhouse," said Scarlett. "I'm going to need to go in, and you have to stay put. No matter what happens."

"What might happen?"

"This is ridiculous," she exclaimed. "Why did I even let you come along with me? You're . . . well, you're you."

"Thanks . . . I think."

"I didn't mean it as a compliment. Listen, Eddie, something is happening in the house down there that is going to change everything, and Cornish is trying to prevent it. When I succeed in stopping him, I may not come back. Do you understand?"

"Not really."

She sighed. "But do you understand that I'm asking you not to follow me?"

"Yes, I understand that."

The rain was taking a break so I lowered my hood, only to feel a huge drop land on my head when we stepped under the trees. I followed Scarlett to a point where we could see the farmhouse she had been talking about.

The walls were covered in ivy, and the brickwork was patchy and old. The whole place looked moldy, neglected, and run-down, but a light on inside indicated it was not as abandoned as it appeared.

"Stupid girl. Why did I come this way?" Scarlett muttered, looking at the steep, muddy slope down to the farmhouse.

"Rascal is managing all right." I pointed out the cat scampering down the hill, then jumping over the stream that ran in front of the house.

"The cat," she whispered. "This is bad."

"You're really worried about the cat, aren't you?"

"The cat couldn't have got out of the car itself, which means someone let it out, which means someone is behind us."

She said it so seriously that it made me want to laugh, but from the way she was looking at me, I didn't think this would go down well.

Then we heard the gunshot.

"Stay here," said Scarlett, and she went skidding, slipping and sliding down the slope, reaching the bottom in seconds. She glanced back up at me, to check that I hadn't followed, then jumped over the stream and went into the farmhouse.

"Stop right there."

The voice came from behind me. I turned and saw the police officer who had come to our school on Thursday.

"Was it you who let Rascal out of the car?" I asked.

"What?"

"The cat."

"Yes. It was an accident," she replied. "My name is PC Liphook. I need to talk to you about the stolen car parked in the field up there. This is very serious, but if you do everything I tell you now, we don't have to make matters any worse. I heard a gunshot."

"Yes, it came from the farmhouse," I said.

"Is that where your girlfriend went?"

"She's not my girlfriend. I do like her and I think she likes me—you know, in an irritated kind of way, but I don't think it's black and white. You know, not like penguins."

"Why are you talking about penguins?"

"It seems to be what I do when I get nervous."

"Is there an easier way down?"

"I don't know. I've never been here before."

I could tell that Liphook was considering the best thing to do next, but the sound of a second gunshot made her spring into action.

"Stay here. Don't move."

She turned and ran along the top of the ridge to find a safer way down. The gunshot echoed around the valley and through my brain. All I could think was that Scarlett was inside that house. I began down the slope but lost my footing almost immediately. I stumbled and slipped. I grabbed a tree trunk and looked down. From this angle, I could see the farmhouse door clearly. The bark of the tree dug into my palm, but the pain vanished as I recognized the dark green door.

I had seen it before. I had stared at that door many times. It was the door from a past I had never known.

It was the door from the photograph of my mother.

CHAPTER 20

THE RECLAMATION OF SENSE

I DON'T KNOW HOW I REACHED THE BOTTOM OF THE slope, but by the time I did, I was wet and muddy. I staggered through the stream to the farmhouse and reached out my hand to the green door. I half believed it to be some kind of mirage that would vanish at my touch, but my fingers connected with it. It felt almost disappointingly real as I pushed it open and heard voices inside.

"You're only making matters worse for yourself, Patrick," said Scarlett.

"This isn't about me," Cornish replied. "My actions are for the greater good."

The door got stuck on a floorboard, but I pushed it harder and stepped into a gloomy room with piles of books everywhere, stacked up like a city skyline. They covered the floor, shelves, and furniture. I could feel the ticklish threat of a sneeze building up in my nose from the dust. Hearing something quietly banging against a door, I pushed it open and saw Rascal in the kitchen, trying to get at a terrified mouse trapped inside a clear plastic mousetrap. The voices were coming from the other side of a door at the far end of the room.

"I'm sorry," said Cornish. "You have left us no choice but to take matters into our own hands."

"Why? Because you disagree with something you don't understand?" said Scarlett.

"We understand that it's wrong to allow the rich to live whatever lives they choose again and again. We understand that echo technology is the single biggest threat to all our futures."

"Patrick, I've seen more of the future than you. Things have changed. There's much more to this than you could ever understand—but, most important, the fact I've jumped back further than you should tell you that this line of action is doomed to failure."

"I don't believe you."

"It's not a case of belief. I promise you that this echo jump has only created a new timeline, and even here, with both Melody and Maguire dead, guess what? Echo technology will still be discovered. You can't stop it."

"We can if we terminate him in the originating timeline."

"It's frightening how little you understand. I'll bet you

don't even know how you ended up here in this version, do you? You jumped back to a world with no Melody. How did that happen?"

"My comrades and I understand enough. We know that this needs to be stopped."

"Patrick, please. Put the gun down."

She said the words calmly, but I felt anything but calm. I rushed to help her, but my foot caught on a pile of books and sent it crashing to the ground, meaning that I fell into the next room and smacked my head on a gray cabinet. I staggered back and saw computers, graphs, strange humming machines, and charts. Cornish was holding an old farmer's shotgun, which he was pointing at Scarlett, who was sitting on the floor, her back against a cabinet like the one I had just head-butted. She held her right hand to her stomach, and I could see dark blood leaking out between her fingers. She looked in a bad way, but not as bad as the man next to her, who was lying facedown, his white lab coat bloodstained and torn by the bullet that had taken his life.

"Eddie, I told you not to come in." Scarlett winced with pain as she spoke.

"You've been shot," I said. In the corner of the room was an overturned chair and camera tripod. I couldn't make sense of any of it.

"This doesn't concern you," she replied.

"Doesn't it?" said Cornish. "Doesn't it concern him more than anyone?"

"No," she said firmly. "Not here. Not this Eddie. What you're doing doesn't make any sense."

"Sense is the thing we're trying to reclaim."

"You can save the speeches and the flawed logic for your hearing."

I couldn't follow much of what they were saying, but I was clear about one thing: we were sharing a room with a dead man, and Cornish had killed him.

"Have you gone mad, sir?" I asked.

"No, Eddie," he said. "I know exactly what I'm doing."

"This is a complicated situation," said Scarlett, "and it's one I need to deal with in accordance with protocols."

"You have protocols for this?" I exclaimed. I was trying not to look at the dead body, but I couldn't tear my eyes away.

"Eddie, you have to get out now," said Scarlett.

"Not without you," I said.

I was trying to stall for time. Any second, I thought, the police officer would be here to sort everything out.

"Patrick, you're leaving me no choice," said Scarlett.

"There's always a choice," said Cornish.

Whatever happened next occurred too fast for me to work out the precise order of events. I could not say if Cornish pulled the trigger before I dived in front of the bullet or if I stepped in his way before he fired at Scarlett. All I knew was the agony of the bullet ripping into my chest.

And the shock.

And the fear.

CHAPTER 21

A NIGHT AT THE HOSPITAL

LIPHOOK HAD HOPED THE MUSEUM WOULD BRING BACK memories, but it had changed too much from the original. The smart museum, with its extensions and explanations, was a far cry from the run-down farmhouse. Besides, her main memory of that long day wasn't the farmhouse but the hospital.

She remembered how Sergeant Copeland had ambled in and immediately made a beeline for the vending machine. It seemed to Liphook that he was very calm, given the situation. It had been his day off, which explained why he was wearing a snug-fitting wool sweater and a pair of shorts.

"Well, Liphook, you did want excitement," he said, pondering which of the chocolate bars on offer was worth his money. "What's the situation, then?"

"One dead, three unconscious," replied Liphook.

"Unconscious?"

"The doctors can't work it out. Two of them have gun-shot wounds, but that doesn't appear to be why they're unconscious. It's like they've fallen asleep with their eyes open. All three are still breathing, but their heart rates are unnaturally slow."

"Sounds a bit peculiar."

"It's very peculiar," said Liphook. "Neither of the gunshot victims sustained serious injuries to the head. The shooter shows no sign of injury at all. And yet it's as though they are all in a coma. Also, two of the victims are minors, sir."

"Children?" said Sergeant Copeland.

"Yes."

Having finally decided on the chocolate bar he wanted, Sergeant Copeland dropped the money into the slot and hit the buttons to extract it. "Do you want anything, Liphook?"

"I would, actually, sir, yes." She chose the biggest bar in the machine, feeling in desperate need of something sweet to replace the bitter aftertaste left by the long wait for the ambulance to arrive, with only the lifeless and wide-eyed bodies for company.

"So, who's who, then?" asked Sergeant Copeland.

"The shooter is called Patrick Cornish. He's an English teacher at Wellcome Valley School."

"That's funny, you were just there the other day, weren't you?"

"Sir, none of this is funny," Liphook said grimly.

"No, of course not. I just meant it was a coincidence. So, an armed English teacher. Who did he shoot?"

"Edward Dane, one of his pupils. He lives with his grandmother, Ruby Dane."

"Yes, I know her," said Sergeant Copeland. "She's a local artist. All those splashes are not to my taste, really, but she's a nice lady."

"She says Eddie sometimes gets a lift home with Mr. Cornish. She has no idea why he stole a car."

"A car theft too? This must feel like Christmas for you," said Sergeant Copeland.

"Christmas usually involves less blood, sir."

"Of course. Yes, of course." Sergeant Copeland laughed awkwardly.

"There was a girl involved in the car theft too. Mrs. Dane has never heard Eddie talk about her, though. She is the other gunshot victim."

"Terrible. A local girl?"

"Actually, no, sir. This is the missing girl we spoke about yesterday, Lauren Bliss. The station is trying to contact her parents."

"How remarkable. What was it? Some kind of Bonnie and Clyde romance?"

"This is where it gets really strange. It seems that Lauren had a second identity. She put on a red wig and caught a train using the name Scarlett White. She arrived here on Wednesday and started school on Thursday."

"What do you mean *started school*? You can't just start school like that." Sergeant Copeland clicked his fingers, forgetting he had been holding a coin and sending it flying across the waiting room.

Liphook explained what she had learned. "A couple calling themselves Mr. and Mrs. White bought a house here in the spring. They applied to the school, and then Scarlett came for an interview back in the summer."

"Have you spoken to them?"

"Yes, sir. The Whites live in Scotland. I managed to establish that they did not buy a house in Wellcome Valley, nor did they come here in the spring. In fact, they had never heard of the place. Also, their daughter Scarlett is not missing."

Sergeant Copeland pulled a biscuit from his top pocket with the flourish of a third-rate magician and looked at it with a satisfied smile. "Identity theft?"

"I believe so, sir, but do you remember how you told me Lauren came here on holiday last summer? The dates coincide with the school interview."

"Remarkable. What about our corpse? How does he fit into this ripe old pick-and-mix bucket?"

"He's the owner of the property. His name is David Maguire. No one knows much about him. Bit of a hermit.

Apparently he used to work at the university as a professor of particle physics, but he lost his job years ago and he's kept to himself ever since."

Seeing a paint-spattered woman enter the waiting room, Sergeant Copeland raised his hand and said, "Hello, Ruby. How are you doing?"

"I've been better, Jim. No one can tell me what's going on."

"I'm so sorry," said Sergeant Copeland. "It is a terrible business. Terrible."

"Yes."

"Can I get you anything?" he asked. "A cup of tea, perhaps?"

"No, thank you." She turned to Liphook. "You asked me if I could think of anything that could explain any of this. There is one thing you should know."

"Yes? What is it?" asked Liphook.

"There's a possibility that David Maguire is Eddie's father."

CHAPTER 22

THURSDAY AGAIN

IT WAS ANOTHER MISERABLE DAY IN THE VALLEY. THE sky was dark and I was as far back in the bus shelter as I could go to avoid the rain. I knew it was the morning because I was dressed for school and waiting for the bus, but what morning was it? How had I got here? I racked my brain for the last thing I could remember.

The bullet.

I placed my hand on the point where it had entered my body. No pain. I pulled up my shirt. There was no wound. No blood.

The arrival of the school bus took me by surprise and showered my legs with puddle water.

"Ready, Eddie?" said Bill. "Then jump on board and hold on steady, Eddie."

I stared back at him. "What day is it?"

"What?"

"Today? What day is it?"

"Thursday," he replied. "Come on, Eddie. I can't stand around discussing days with you. We've got places to go."

I got onto the bus and sat down next to Angus. "Morning, Eddie," he said. "Anything amazing to report?"

"What?" I said.

"Anything amazing since yesterday?" he said.

"What day was yesterday?" I asked.

"Are you all right?"

"I don't know. What day was yesterday?"

"Yesterday was Wednesday. Today is Thursday. I imagine tomorrow will be Friday."

"What happened to midterm break?"

"That's next week."

"What? It's the Thursday before? Hold on, is this a joke?"

"You tell me," said Angus. "You're the one saying all this stuff."

"So, you're telling me that today is two days ago, tomorrow is yesterday, and what was today hasn't happened yet?"

Angus gave me a small round of applause. "Very good."

"I'm serious," I said. "What's going on?"

Angus looked around him and said in his best Sherlock Holmes voice, "It appears to be some kind of school bus. It's morning and we're wearing school uniforms, and therefore, Watson, I conclude that we are going to school."

"But I've done all this before," I said.

"Oh, I get it," said Angus. "This is the old *we've done this before* routine. Very good."

All around me, I could see the same people in the same seats, having the same conversations. Angus drew a face in the condensation. The lips dripped down and made it look like a vampire, just as before. We were approaching the spot where we picked up Scarlett, but Bill wasn't slowing down.

I stood up. "Hey."

"No standing on the bus," shouted Bill.

"You didn't stop for her," I yelled.

"Who?" replied Bill.

"Scarlett."

"Who's Scarlett?" asked Angus.

"She . . . she lives . . . Well, I don't know where she lives, but he's supposed to stop for her and she's supposed to get on. That's what happens. That's what happened before."

"Now, Eddie, I'm not saying I'm not enjoying this, but there is a tiny element of it that is a little bit mental."

"I've been here before," I said. "I've already lived through this day."

"Great. So, what's going to happen then?" said Angus.

"Er . . ." I had to think. Apart from Scarlett arriving, what had happened on Thursday? "We're going to have a police talk from an officer called . . . called . . . What's her name?" It seemed ridiculous that I could have forgotten,

but the more I tried to access it, the further it retreated to the back of my mind.

"You should be careful how you use such a precious gift," said Angus. "You have obviously been given great knowledge."

I ran through everything I could tell him that would convince him, but once you removed Scarlett, what was there? Should I tell him about the lessons we would sit through or who would get told off for talking? I couldn't think of anything that he couldn't put down to a lucky guess.

"So, great and noble time traveler," said Angus, "tell us about the future. Are there flying cars? Please say there are flying cars."

"By Saturday? Funnily enough, no, although there is a stolen car with a cat in the back."

"It's a start, I suppose."

23

SAME OLD, SAME OLD

THE STRANGEST THING ABOUT RELIVING THAT MORN-
ing was how it didn't feel all that strange. I had spent my
life reliving the same day over and over, listening to the
same names being read off the register by our teacher,
then filing in and out of the same lessons.

This was only different because it was *exactly* the same.
I studied each repetition with interest. I tried to recall the
exact details, but a lot of what I saw and heard was new to
me. I was beginning to realize how little I listened.

On the way into the auditorium, the police officer
caught my eye and, for a fleeting moment, I thought she
recognized me, but she looked away and I understood that
we were strangers.

Seeing Mrs. Lewis stand up, we fell quiet, and she said,
"Now, everyone, we have a very special guest, so let's show

her what a polite and well-behaved school we are as we welcome Officer Liphook."

It was more obvious to me this time how nervous she was.

"*Community*," she began. "Who can tell me what that word means?"

I glanced around. Was I really the only one who had heard all this before? I was still half expecting everyone to start laughing and reveal that it was all an elaborate joke.

"Looking out for each other."

Two rows in front of me, a girl played with her friend's hair before a warning look from a teacher stopped her.

"Being selfless."

Along my row, a boy fiddled with a grubby tissue, dropped it, picked it up, then used it to wipe his nose.

"Sticking to the rules."

Why was I back here? Had I been shot dead? Was this what happened after death? Were the dead forced to relive the last few days of their lives—and if that was the case, why wasn't Scarlett here?

Scarlett, I thought. She was the key. Her absence was the main difference, as far as I could tell. If she wasn't here, then I wasn't reliving the exact same day after all. I was reliving a different version of it. I remembered her saying something to Cornish about different versions back at the farmhouse. What did any of it mean, and how was I supposed to make sense of it?

"Eddie Dane," said Mrs. Lewis. "Have you a question for Officer Liphook?"

Everyone turned to look at me. It took me a moment to realize why. I had my hand up. I think I had been trying to prove to myself that I could do things differently.

"What's your question?" asked PC Liphook.

I had sat through the same speech twice, yet I had no idea what she had been saying. "I have a question about car theft," I said. It was the first thing that came to mind.

"Yes? What is it?"

I wondered if PC Liphook actually looked grateful for the interruption.

"Er, how serious a crime is it?"

"Very serious," replied PC Liphook.

Mrs. Lewis was giving me a warning stare, but I continued. "What's worse: stealing a car, breaking into a house, driving without a license, or accidentally kidnapping a cat?"

The question got a big laugh and a thumbs-up from Angus but a threatening snarl from Mrs. Lewis.

"That's quite a list," said PC Liphook. "May I ask the reason for your question?"

Mrs. Lewis answered for me. "Sorry, Officer Liphook, you appear to be the unlucky recipient of one of Eddie's jokes."

"It's not a joke," I said. "I'm interested. I mean, what if the keys were left in the car?"

"That's enough," said Mrs. Lewis.

"It's all right," said PC Liphook. "I can answer that one. Opportunity is not an excuse. It is a reason. Most crimes are opportunistic. That doesn't make them any less serious. And murder is the most serious crime of all, because . . ."

"It involves removing a person's life, which can't be replaced," I said. "You've already told us that."

"Have I?" She looked confused.

She had not. Not on this Thursday.

Mrs. Lewis was on her feet again. "I think, Eddie, that rather than second-guessing what our guest is going to say, maybe you should try listening. With your ears. At the end, I'm sure PC Liphook will happily take your questions."

"Er . . ." Liphook looked down at her notes and flicked through several cards, then said, "Maybe this is a good time for questions."

She picked the first hand to go up. "Yes, what's your question?"

"Have you ever shot anyone?"

24

MONSTROUS THINGS

IT WAS JUST A GAME FOR ANGUS.

"It's good, this *I've been here before* stuff," he said, chewing a meatball.

I had spent the morning making predictions about lesson subjects and who would get told off for what, but it was hardly proof.

"I didn't fully get the thing you did in assembly, if I'm honest," said Angus, "but it was still funny."

"It wasn't meant to be funny," I said.

"What did we talk about last time we were here, then?"

"Meatballs," I replied, "and how they want to be eaten."

Angus laughed. "Hold on. Was that meant to be funny?"

"I don't know."

Angus skewered another meatball with his fork. "It's interesting, though, this whole act, because it kind of shows how predictable everything is."

"I suppose."

Without Scarlett, the afternoon dragged until finally we reached the last lesson. English. I watched Cornish bustle around the room and remembered the look of hatred in his eyes as he fired the gun.

"Monsters," he said. "I want us to name as many monsters as we can, comrades."

I was surprised when I heard my own voice answer. "You."

"Are you calling me a monster, Eddie?" He sounded amused.

"I . . . No . . . I meant humans."

Cornish twisted around on his heel. "Interesting answer, Eddie," he said. "Why?"

"Because humans do monstrous things. Humans make guns. Humans shoot people." I don't know what had taken control of me. What could I possibly hope to achieve?

"It's true, guns are a monstrous invention," he agreed. "They turn those who use them into monsters."

"So, what would it take?" I asked. "I mean, for you to fire a gun at someone? For you to kill?"

"I hope I never find out," said Cornish, "but to answer your question, I would do all I could to avoid using violence, but if it came to it and if the cause justified it, yes, I think I would pick up a gun. Thankfully, we can choose not to be monsters. We have free will, which brings us to the book we will be looking at for the next few weeks."

When he distributed the books, I got the same copy with the picture of the yellow-faced old man on the cover.

"Why are these books all different? Mine's falling apart," complained the same girl as before.

"Don't panic, comrades, they all have the same words on the inside."

"But we all know this story," said Angus.

"You mean you know what happens," said Cornish. "That isn't the same as knowing the story. And I will want the books back at the end of the term, so please treat them with respect."

He snatched the same book from the same girl.

"So, can anyone tell me this book's alternative title?"

"*The Modern Prometheus*," said a voice behind me.

For one hopeful moment I thought it was Scarlett, but I turned to find that it was another girl in my class who had spoken.

"Very good," said Cornish.

"It's printed on the front of my book," replied the girl. "Who's Prometheus, then?"

"Prometheus is from Greek mythology," explained Cornish. "He created humans from clay, then brought his creation to life with fire stolen from the gods. You see, comrades, ever since we crawled out of the primordial sludge, humans have created imaginary monsters . . ."

The rest of Cornish's speech was little more than background noise, drowned out by the confused thoughts racing through my head as I tried to understand what was happening to me.

25

LAUREN BLISS

THAT NIGHT, LAUREN BLISS WAS THE FIRST TO COME out of the coma. Her parents were still on their way, so Liphook went in alone to talk to her.

"Where am I?" Lauren's blond hair had been flattened by the red wig. She looked scared and tired and extremely confused.

Liphook sat down by her bed. "You're in the hospital. You're fine, but you have been shot."

"Shot? With a gun, shot?"

Liphook nodded. "Yes. Earlier today. Do you remember what happened?"

"No."

"Do you remember why you were wearing this wig?" She picked it up from the bedside table.

"No. This doesn't make any sense. Where are my parents?"

"They're on their way. They'll be here soon."

"Where am I?"

"Wellcome Valley Hospital."

"Wellcome Valley? That's not possible."

"You put on this wig and caught a train here. You pretended your name was Scarlett White. Are you telling me you don't remember any of this?" Liphook had decided against making notes, but now she wondered if she should be treating this as an official statement after all and took out her notebook.

"I don't remember a thing," said Lauren.

"You don't remember stealing a car with your boyfriend?"

"My boyfriend?" Lauren sat up and looked at the boy lying in the bed next to her. "Who is he?"

"His name is Eddie."

"The last thing I remember, I was at home."

"But you have been to the valley before, yes? You came during the summer."

"Yes, Mum and Dad rented a holiday cottage. It was nice."

"Did you meet Eddie then?"

"I didn't meet anyone. I don't think I met anyone. Maybe I did. I don't know. Every time I try to remember, I get this burning pain in my head. What does it mean? What's happening to me?"

Liphook wrote down *Memory loss.*

CHAPTER 26

REALITY AND EMOTIONS

MAYBE I HAD BEEN LOOKING AT THINGS THE WRONG way. Instead of trying to spot similarities, should I have been looking for the differences? How was this Thursday different from the last one? Apart from Scarlett's absence, the main difference was my behavior. If I tried to do things the same as last time, maybe I would be able to see what else had changed. So when Cornish asked me if I wanted a lift home, I said, "Thanks."

"How about you, Angus?" he said.

"I'm getting picked up by the noise-mobile," replied Angus.

"Just you and me, then, Eddie," he said. "I'll see you by the car once I'm done here."

I followed Angus out into the drizzly car park.

"So, what happens now, future man?" he asked.

"Your mum comes to pick you up. She parks outside the

gates and flashes her headlights. One of the twins opens a door but she yells at the wrong one while the baby screams his head off. After you've gone, Cornish comes out, only he's forgotten who I am."

"That sounds like a fun trip home for the both of us, then."

"Last call for anywhere but here," yelled Bill, closing the bus doors.

"Never gets old," I said.

The car's headlights flashed and the door opened, releasing the noise from within. Angus looked impressed. "I'll see you tomorrow," he said. I watched him run to his car.

The other thought that had occurred to me was that this was a dream, but it didn't feel like a dream. It was too plodding. Too slow. Too real. All of which left only one explanation: I had traveled back in time.

"Hi, Eddie." Mr. Cornish jangled his keys. "Get in, then."

I stared back at him. "You remember you're giving me a lift, sir?" I said.

He laughed. "I'm not that old," he replied.

I got into the car.

"You were quick with that monster question," he said. "I was expecting a whole list before we got to humans."

"Sorry, sir."

He laughed. "Don't apologize for being smart, Eddie."

There was no confusion this time as he slipped the car into gear and reversed out of the space.

"Sir, can I ask you something? Do you believe in time travel?"

He thought before replying. "I certainly believe that books can transport us back in time, yes. I think that memories can be triggered by our senses. I have experienced déjà vu—that's thinking you've visited a place before when you haven't. But do I believe it is possible to transport a human back in time? No."

"Why not?"

"Because if anyone had invented time travel, someone would have come back and told us about it."

"Perhaps they're not allowed to. Perhaps there are protocols."

"Protocols," repeated Cornish with a smile. "I like that. Are you writing a story about this?"

"No."

"Maybe you should. Writing helps, you know."

"Helps what, sir?"

"It helps you tackle problems. It helps you figure out how you feel."

I didn't know what to say to this, so I didn't say anything.

"I'm sorry," he said. "I don't mean to be insensitive, but you should understand that feelings are complicated for everyone. It's all right to feel sad sometimes. I know you like to make jokes and pretend everything is fine, but you can talk to me about things anytime you want."

"You're talking about Melody," I said.

"You can tell me to shut up if you like."

"Actually, I think this does have something to do with her."

"The time-travel story?"

Cornish hadn't attempted to turn the radio on this time, so the only sounds, apart from our voices, were those of the wheels on the road, the rain on the roof, and the swish of the windscreen wipers.

"It's not a story. It's something real that is happening to me, and I think it has something to do with her."

He considered this. "Emotions are real."

"I'm not talking about emotions. I'm talking about the fact that I've lived through this day already, and I'm scared about what it means."

"Life can be scary," he agreed.

There was no point. No one was going to help me understand.

"Are you going to try to read the book, then, do you think?" he asked.

"I might. Do you know which chapter has Frankenstein making the monster?"

"Chapter five," he replied. "Why?"

"I was thinking I might just skip to that bit."

He laughed. "Why on earth would you do that?"

"Because that's where it gets interesting."

27

HISTORY MATTERS

THE FIRST THING I DID WHEN I GOT HOME WAS GO INTO the kitchen to turn off the stove, then pick up a dustpan and broom. I went into the living room and switched on the light.

"Too bright," said Ruby.

I cleaned up the glass, then carefully tipped it into the bin and sat down at the kitchen table with the photograph. All my life, this picture had been my only window into the past. I knew every detail of it, from the watchband on my mother's wrist to the missing button on her dungarees. I stared at that closed green door—not of some far-flung holiday cottage but of an old farmhouse right here in the valley. Finally I had stepped into this picture, so why was I even more confused than before?

Ruby joined me in the kitchen and looked at the photograph in my hand. "Sorry, lad. I had one of my moments."

"You always said you didn't know where it was taken," I said.

"Yes. Maybe she was on holiday."

"Who with?"

"Oh, Eddie, I can't remember." Ruby held her hand to her temple to show that I was giving her a headache.

"I don't believe you."

"Please . . ."

"You have one photo of your daughter. Just one. And you don't know where it was taken or who took it?"

"Photographs aren't real. They only show—"

"What things look like on the outside," I interrupted. "Except that's not true. This shows more. I'm on the inside in this picture. You can't see me but you know I'm there. You also know that there must be someone holding the camera. Who is she smiling at? Who took it?"

"I'm sorry, Eddie. I can't do this now. Not today." She turned to leave.

"I've been there. I've seen this door." I could feel the anger simmering inside of me.

She stopped but avoided my gaze. "Was he there?" she asked quietly.

"Who?"

"It doesn't matter. Don't go back, please."

"Why? Who lives there?"

"There's nothing for you there. I imagine he's moved now, anyway."

"Who?"

"No one important."

"Who?"

Tense music played from the living room as a contestant reached the final sudden-death round.

"Please stay away from there," said Ruby. "Please. For me."

"Who lives there?"

"I can't . . ."

"What was his name?"

I had lived through enough of Ruby's down days to know how to make her answer. Once my insistent nagging had worked its way inside her head and become a part of the pain that was already there, she would do anything to make it stop.

"His name is David Maguire. He was your mother's lecturer at university, but that was a long time ago. Can we drop this now? It's history."

"You say that like history doesn't matter."

"Of course it matters, but there's nothing we can do about it." Ruby sighed. "I understand that you want to find something else. I know ours is not much of a life. Maybe we'll do better next time, eh, lad? But you won't find any solutions buried in the past."

She walked back to watch the end of the quiz show, leaving me alone with my thoughts.

CHAPTER 28

THE TIME PARTICLE

I UNPLUGGED THE PHONE BEFORE LEAVING THE HOUSE because, although I was wearing my uniform and carrying my bag, I had no intention of catching the bus this Friday and I didn't want Ruby to worry when the school called home.

It felt good to take matters into my own hands. If I had to relive this day, I would do it on my own terms. I had slept badly the previous night, having been kept awake by my endlessly spiraling thoughts. As I cycled up the hill, I lost myself to the turn of the wheels, the coldness of the rain, and the burning of my leg muscles. I took the same route to the farmhouse that I had taken with Scarlett. As I wheeled my bike along the muddy path, it struck me that Scarlett had said there was probably a better way to get there, but it was too late to turn back.

At the end of the field, I found a safer way down. I was

in no rush this time. My head was filled with the dark, bloodstained memory of the last time I had been there, but how could you remember something that was yet to happen?

I stopped outside the door. The rain was still coming down hard, so I had to be careful taking the photograph out of the book. I held it up, but I didn't need proof. I knew it was the same one. The photographer had stood on the other side of the stream, while my mother squinted in the sunlight. It was such a stark contrast to the dark skies above me that it felt like another world entirely.

I knocked on the door.

"Who is it?" shouted a voice.

It was a simple enough question, but what was my answer?

"My name's Eddie," I said.

"If you are here to sell something, I'm not interested."

"I think you knew my mother, Melody Dane."

There was a pause, followed by the voice saying, "Hold on."

I heard locks being unlocked and bolts sliding to the side. When the door opened, it caught on the uneven floorboard.

"Give it a push, will you?"

I pushed and the door swung open to reveal a messy-haired man wearing a white lab coat. I had seen him before, only the last time he had been lying on the floor, dead. Very much alive now, he narrowed his keen eyes with interest as he inspected me.

"You're Melody's son?" he said.

"Yes," I replied.

There was something unnerving about the way he looked at me. In spite of the rain, he didn't ask me in.

"Are you David Maguire?" I asked.

"Er, yes . . ."

I showed him the photograph. "Did you take this?"

He stared at it for a couple of seconds, then nodded, although I had to wonder if he was responding to me, or to some other unheard question. "Why are you here?" he asked.

"Can I come in?" I said.

He moved out of the way and I stepped into the room full of books. I placed the photograph back between the pages of *Frankenstein* and dropped it into my bag.

"You taught Melody at university," I said.

"Yes, your mother was very bright. The brightest. Her death was, well, it was unfortunate." He bent down to pick up one of the clear plastic mousetraps and check whether it had caught anything. Finding it empty, he placed it back on the floor.

"Can I ask what you do here?" I said.

"Nothing you could possibly understand," he replied. "Sorry, why are you here?"

"I've been here before," I said.

"I know. She brought you here as a baby."

"I don't mean that," I began. "Hold on, I thought Melody dropped out of university after she had me. Why would she come here?"

"She came here to help out with my project, but this is all a very long time ago. I fail to see what it has to do with anything."

"The last time I came here was tomorrow," I said.

Maguire looked at me with curiosity. "Tomorrow?"

"I can't explain it, but I've lived through this day."

"Oh, I see," said Maguire. "This is a joke, is it?"

"No."

"I'm afraid you have got the wrong end of the stick, young man. I may tick all the boxes required for a crazy rogue scientist inventing a time machine, but you have obviously failed to grasp the complexity of my work here."

"Your work?"

I followed Maguire into the lab, careful this time to avoid the stacks of books as I entered the brightly lit room filled with computer screens and scientific equipment.

"What is all this stuff?" I asked.

"It's a particle accelerator," he replied. "It isolates sub-atomic particles and enables me to manipulate them. It has been built with the specific purpose of studying the time particle, which is presumably the reason for your time-travel joke."

"What's a time particle?"

"To answer that, you must first ask what is time."

"I don't know," I said.

"Of course you don't. Physicists have wrestled with this question for many years. The general belief is that time is a dimension that we travel through, but this is incorrect. Time is a force that acts upon us, like gravity. It is a physical law that we must obey, and the things that govern that relationship are known as time particles. They exist within us and all around us. They regulate our relationship with time, ensuring that we move forward at a constant rate."

I was trying to keep up, but Maguire didn't seem especially interested in whether I was following or not.

"Seconds, minutes, hours, days, months, and years are the measurements we use for time, created in accordance with the specific movements of our planet and sun. The time particle, however, is not unique to our position in the galaxy. It is a universal necessity. It is a requirement for existence, just as water is a prerequisite for life."

"So, what's it look like?"

"It doesn't look like anything. We are talking about something so small it couldn't be seen even with the most powerful magnification. This equipment enables me to monitor these particles, not see them. It stands to reason, you see, that if the time particle can be isolated, it can be manipulated, and thus our relationship with time can be altered."

"But aren't you talking about time travel?"

"No, I am not," he snapped.

"But—"

"Let me explain it." Maguire grabbed a clipboard and blank piece of paper. He drew a line. "Look. We know that time moves in one direction, which is why we remember the past but we do not remember the future. In that sense, we are all traveling through time, because we are traveling forward at a constant rate governed by the time particle. To travel backward, however, would involve moving to an earlier point." He drew a loop to indicate this.

"Yes, exactly—"

"But the very act of making this jump would necessarily cause a split in the timeline." He drew a second line coming off the first that connected with the loop. "However, the first line would also have to remain for the jump to be possible. This would involve the duplication of every molecule in the universe, creating at least two separate strands of existence. There is no evidence to suggest that this is possible, and that is not what I am trying to do here."

He hastily scribbled over the lines, tore the paper off the clipboard, crumpled it up, and threw it away.

"So, what is all this stuff for, then?"

"The isolation of the time particle will enable an alteration of our relationship with time."

"Meaning?"

"Imagine if you could slow down time so that a second lasted an hour or speed it up so that a day vanished in the blink of eye. Time particle acceleration will change how we experience time, in much the same way that the invention of the steam train or air travel altered our relationship with distance. The development of faster transportation made the world a smaller place. My invention will do the same for time. We will be able to control time."

"But what's all this got to do with my mother?"

"Melody was instrumental in the formulation of this idea. She believed in me when others did not. If she had lived, I have no doubt she would have remained involved with this project. I owe her a great debt, and finally, after many years, I am almost at the point of completion."

"You mean you can now slow down time?" I said.

"Any day now. What a coincidence that you should show up now at the final stages of the project your mother helped start, but I suppose it was inevitable that you would turn up at some point."

"Inevitable how?"

He didn't answer the question, instead finding a computer screen that urgently required his attention.

"Look, I'm not very good at this sort of thing. Feelings and . . . you know . . . emotions."

"What are you talking about?" I asked.

"What has Ruby told you?" he said.

"Very little except to stay away."

"She said the same to me. She made it very clear after

your mother's death that I was not welcome. I suppose she blamed me."

"Blamed you? For what?"

"For Melody's death. It was my car she was driving, you see, and if we hadn't argued, she would never have been out on such a stormy night. Perhaps Ruby was right to hold me responsible."

"I thought her argument was with Ruby."

"Your mother was capable of arguing with more than one person at a time. She was very intelligent, but she was not the easiest of people."

"What were you arguing about?" I asked.

"I told her that she should go back and finish her degree, that she shouldn't let a child get in the way of her career. She thought I was . . ." Maguire looked at me and his words faded away. "Anyway, she shouldn't have been driving that night. Especially not with a child in the back. It was typically irresponsible of her."

"What child?"

"You, of course," he said plainly. "Oh, you didn't know? I'm sorry. I did tell you that I'm not much good at this sort of thing."

CHAPTER 29

TEMPORAL COMA

I DIDN'T UNDERSTAND WHY RUBY HAD LIED TO ME, BUT Maguire was not especially interested in the subject. He busied himself in the lab, apparently unaware of the impact of his words on me. There was something strangely detached about the man. Hearing a noise in the other room, he dashed out, only to return with a mouse trapped inside one of the clear plastic boxes. He placed it on a wooden chair and pointed a huge telescope-like thing at it. He then adjusted a few dials, checked all the monitors, and made several notes on his clipboard, all the time muttering to himself.

"What are you going to do to the mouse?" I asked.

"You're not one of those animal rights people, are you?" he said.

"No, but—"

"Good."

"Are you going to hurt it?"

"I have no reason to believe that the process will have any effect on its nerve endings. I'll be altering its time perception, so no, it shouldn't experience any pain."

"Why?"

"Rodent testing is necessary for me to ensure that all aspects are accounted for before I move on to the first human experiment."

"But why mess about with time, anyway? What's the point?"

He paused to consider this question as though it wasn't something that had occurred to him. "The furtherance of science, primarily," he said, "but one can perceive of practical applications . . . Imagine if you could, I don't know, dodge a bullet . . . or have more time to stop the spread of a disease before it became an epidemic. Millions of lives could be saved. But let me get on . . . Oh, the camera. I almost forgot the camera." He darted back out and returned with a small video camera, which he attached to a wobbly tripod. He aimed the camera at the mouse and fiddled to get it into focus.

It was the same camera and chair that I had seen on my previous visit. The mouse desperately and hopelessly searched for a way out of the trap, while Maguire made a few final adjustments.

"The accelerator will first isolate our subject's governing time particles," he said.

He flicked various switches. I was half expecting a flash of lightning or a huge laser beam to shoot from the end, but instead the machine made a slightly louder buzzing noise, and the mouse quivered in fear.

"Look here." Maguire pointed at a computer screen full of white dots. Every few seconds the screen refreshed, showing that the dots had moved. "Each one of those dots represents a time particle," he said. "I will now establish which of these control the rodent's temporal movement."

The machine beeped and Maguire spent several minutes scribbling down things on his piece of paper. "Yes. Got them."

He went back to the main machine and typed a few numbers. "Having isolated them, we now accelerate the time particles."

"You mean, you make them go faster?"

He looked annoyed by the question. "No. We are essentially copying particles, then firing them back at themselves. Without a PhD in particle physics, you stand very little chance of understanding this. Even with one, you'd struggle. Now, please be quiet."

The telescope-like thing moved closer to the petrified mouse.

"Isn't the plastic in the way?" I asked.

Maguire shook his head. "I am dealing with things a million times smaller than an atom. Now, watch what happens to the rodent when its time particles are accelerated."

One of the machines made a kind of ticking noise, and the mouse went rigid and keeled over.

"You've killed it!" I exclaimed.

"No," said Maguire. "He's not dead. This monitor is measuring the mouse's heartbeat. Normally that would be around six hundred and seventy beats per minute, but this little rodent's rate has slowed down to the speed of a blue whale's."

Peering closely, I could see that the mouse's eyes were wide open.

"What's happening to him?"

"His temporal readings indicate that his perception of time is being altered. He's in what I call a *temporal coma*. The problem, of course, is that I can't ask him what he is experiencing, which is why I need to move on and test it on myself."

The rigid mouse was a horrific sight. "You're going to do that to yourself?"

"Once all the teething problems have been eradicated, yes."

"What problems?"

A machine beeped. "Watch. He's about to come out of the coma. This bit is fascinating."

The mouse twitched and very suddenly began to move. It ran around the inside of the trap, making a terrible high-pitched squealing noise, then suddenly scrunched up into a ball.

"Has it gone back into the coma?" I asked.

"No. It's dead now," said Maguire.

"I thought you said you weren't going to hurt it."

"I didn't hurt it, but the process is not properly refined yet. The mice are still experiencing some kind of brain overload, which kills them the moment they return to their originating point in time."

"So, you've killed lots of mice."

He sighed. "These rodents are dying in the name of science. We all should hope for such a noble death."

30

POSSIBILITY OF PARENTHOOD

"MAY I SEE THE PHOTOGRAPH AGAIN?" ASKED MAGUIRE.

I reached into my bag and pulled out the book.

"*Frankenstein*," he said. "Interesting choice."

"We're doing it at school."

"It was one of Melody's favorite books, if my memory serves me right. Her copy is here somewhere, along with all her other books."

I handed him the photograph.

"They're her books? Why are they here?" I asked.

"She left them here. I've been meaning to throw them out. Perhaps you want them? You could take them with you. Personally, I've never seen the point in fiction. There are enough true things to learn without filling one's head with made-up stories."

"But why did she leave them here in the first place?"

Maguire handed the picture back to me. "I remember

that day," he said. "We had just begun work on the first of this machine's many predecessors."

"Why are my mother's books here?"

Maguire shifted awkwardly. "You should probably speak to Ruby about that."

"About what?"

"It's not really for me to say these things."

"What things?"

"Besides, I did suggest we find out," he said. "I thought that if we had a definitive answer on your parentage, then it might be better for everyone."

"What are you talking about?"

"The possibility of me being your father," he said, "although Melody never furnished me with the exact percentage of that possibility."

"My father?"

"Your mother was always extremely evasive on the subject."

"No one told me."

"Yes, I can see that."

"Ruby always said she didn't know anything about my dad."

"*Dad* is a word generally associated with close familial contact. We are talking about biological parentage and the likelihood that I am genetically responsible for your existence. Whatever the truth, I'm not dad material."

I could hear him talking in his detached tone of voice,

but as I listened, my thoughts became tangled up with
my memories. I knew I had no memory of my mother, so
why could I now picture her face? Why did this feel like a
conversation we had had before? I remembered Cornish
talking about déjà vu. Is that what this was?

The world suddenly felt very unstable, and I lost my bal-
ance. I staggered into the chair and sent the dead mouse
flying off. I knocked something over. It was an old farmer's
shotgun that had been leaning against the wall behind the
door. It was the same one Cornish had been holding. I
felt a shooting pain in my head. I could tell that Maguire
was kneeling down in front of me saying something, but it
wasn't his voice I could hear.

"*Come on, lad, snap out of this.*" It was Ruby. "*You've frightened us all enough now. Please, wake up, Eddie.*"

I could hear her but I could not see her. When I closed
my eyes, I saw Maguire lying dead in the pool of blood.
He turned to look at me, and his cold, dead lips moved,
as though he was trying to tell me something. I wanted
to scream but I didn't know how. The pool of red liquid
was spreading toward me, but it dripped away before it
reached me, taking the memory with it.

I was back in the room with Maguire leaning over me,
looking concerned.

"You appear to have fainted," he said.

"Get off me."

I pushed him back and ran out of the room, but forgot

about the books and sent a pile flying. When I reached the front door, I glanced over my shoulder. Maguire was watching me with a look of mild curiosity, but my eyes were drawn to the cover of one of the books I had knocked over. It was a black hardback with the word *FRANKENSTEIN* printed in gold capital letters on the front.

31

THE UGLINESS OF REGRET

WHAT ELSE HAD RUBY LIED ABOUT? SHE WAS HONEST enough about how terrible it was to be lumbered with me, so why had she avoided telling me about Maguire or the truth about Melody's accident?

Lost in thought as I pedaled down the road, I didn't see the truck until it was almost upon me. It sounded its horn and I swerved to the side. I must have hit a stone because I went flying off my bike and landed on the shoulder. The driver didn't stop to check whether I was all right. I sat on the grass. My heart pounded. I looked over the edge and imagined a stormy night and my mother driving fast with me in the backseat.

I liked the feeling of the rain on my face and the damp ground beneath my hands because it reminded me that this was real. I checked my bike. It was undamaged, so I got back on.

It was lunchtime when I reached the school gates. I stood behind the thin wire fence, watching the first shift go into the hall.

Among the many thoughts that twisted through my mind was the vision of that mouse's wide eyes. Awake but unaware. What horror had that rodent lived through before its death? I ran my fingers over my face, trying to understand what was happening to me. Why, when I looked up at the sky, did it seem as white as a hospital ceiling? Where did that thought even come from? I had no memory of ever having been in a hospital, but if Maguire had been telling the truth, surely I would have been taken to one after the crash? Was it that memory that I was now accessing?

I saw Angus in the canteen window, looking at me. He raised a hand to wave. I quickly jumped back on my bike.

The rest of the day was lost in the rain and the endless turning of the bicycle wheels. When I finally got home, I opened the door and heard Ruby's crackly jazz record playing. Chaotic, tuneless sounds. I looked at Ruby's painting.

"What do you think?" she asked.

"I don't know," I replied.

She pushed her paintbrush into her hair and turned to look at me. "Is everything all right, Eddie?"

"Is he my father?" I said.

Ruby sat down. "You've been to see him." She sighed. "That's why you weren't at school."

"How do you know I wasn't?"

"I plugged the phone in. Don't worry. I covered for you and said you were sick."

I was too angry to feel grateful. "He told me I was in the car when Melody crashed."

"Of course he did."

"Is it true?"

"Truth." I hated Ruby's smile at that moment. "Is that what you're after?"

"I want to know what happened."

"Knowing what happened isn't the same as knowing the truth."

"Just tell me."

Ruby walked to the record player and turned it down. "Yes, you were in the car. Yes, Maguire is probably your father."

"Why didn't you tell me?"

"I didn't tell you about Maguire because your mother made it extremely clear that he had no claim over you. I thought he deserved to know whether he was your father or not, but she didn't want him to have anything to do with your upbringing."

"So, you lied to me."

"The world is held together by lies. When I paint, I'm

searching for the truth in between them, but I'm no better at this than anyone else. Worse, probably."

"I'm not talking about your stupid painting!" I shouted.

Ruby pulled the paintbrush from her hair and dropped it into a jar of discolored water. "Do you really want to know why I kept the truth from you all these years about you being in the back of that car?"

"Yes."

"Because once I tell you, you can't be untold."

"I want to know the truth."

"The truth is, I couldn't bear to tell you that when your mother decided to kill herself, she also tried to take you with her."

"Kill herself?" It was all I could say.

"Things were not good between her and David. After you were born, she was lower than I had ever seen her. She had given up her studies. She was stuck here with me and with you."

"So?"

"Eddie, Melody knew that road as well as anyone."

"You're saying she drove off it on purpose with me in the back?" I said.

"I don't know. I used to think that. It doesn't matter. It doesn't change anything."

Ruby placed a hand on my arm, but I shook her off me.

"I'm sorry, lad. I really am."

She turned the volume back up on the record player,

filling the room with chaos. I looked at her painting. The splashes and strokes of random colors began to move in front of my eyes, forming shapes and scenes. I saw a face. I saw the curve of a road and the swirling patterns of a storm cloud. None of these images lasted more than a second, but each left a deep imprint on my eyes.

"It's regret," said Ruby.

"It's horrible," I said.

32

THE LOVE OF HEIGHTS

BETWEEN RUBY'S JAZZ AND THE CONFUSION IN MY head, I didn't know how long the phone had been ringing by the time I heard it. I pushed the living room door shut and picked up the receiver. From the screaming and shouting on the other end, I knew it was Angus before he spoke.

"Shut up! I'm on the phone," I heard him yell.

"Mum, Angus told me to shut up," responded one of the twins.

"Angus, please don't tell your brother to shut up," shouted his mother.

"Sorry, Eddie. It's all gone mad here," said Angus. "Where were you today?"

"Off sick," I said.

"Off sick, sick?" he responded. "Or, you know, *sick* sick?"

"What sort of sick is it if you're actually visiting someone who tells you he might be your father?"

"I'm not sure there's a word for that."

"Angus," I said, "you know how we make everything into a joke?"

"Yes, I like that about us."

"What if it's not? What if it's serious?"

"Are you all right, Eddie?"

I wanted to tell him everything I had learned about Maguire and Melody and the accident, but I didn't know how. Most of the time, Angus and I said things to make each other laugh. We didn't talk about real stuff. If this even was real stuff.

"I'm fine," I said.

"Was it you I saw outside at lunchtime?" he asked.

"I don't know." It was true. I didn't know. Had I stood outside the school at lunchtime, or had I been at school all day? My voice wavered as I said, "I think I might have gone mad."

"Didn't that happen years ago?" asked Angus. "Now, are you still up for the project tomorrow?"

"What project?"

"The Ten Tops Challenge. The trees."

"Oh, that. What's the point?"

Angus didn't reply immediately, but when he did, he said, "You want to know the point? Tomorrow morning, I'll most probably be woken up by one of the twins throwing the other onto my face. After that, my day will involve screaming, punching, puking, lots of shouting, and unfair blaming, then door slamming and, finally, more screaming."

I laughed.

"But once we get up that first tree, Eddie, there's none of that. It's just you and me. You know when you're right up high and you realize it's windier up there than it is down below and the branch is swinging forward and back? Great big swings and you just have to cling on until it stops? And you feel dizzy and terrified and just brilliant? I love that."

"I hate that," I said.

"I love it because you've got no control over what happens, but at the same time it's up to you not to let go. Isn't that the point of doing anything, to feel like that?"

"I don't know the point of anything. Remember, I've gone mad."

"Well, I'm completing this project whether you're with me or not. These trees need climbing, and I'm going to climb them. I'll see you tomorrow, okay?"

"It's going to rain tomorrow," I said.

"It's not supposed to. Hold on, someone's shouting for me. I'M ON THE PHONE! Listen, Eddie, I've got to go. World War Three is breaking out."

Angus hung up and I started up the stairs, but Ruby appeared at the living room door.

"Are we still arguing?" she asked.

"Not if it means you'll leave me alone," I replied.

"Come on, lad. I can't change what's already done, and

I wouldn't change my part in it if I could. How could anyone tell a child those things?"

"How could anyone keep it a secret?"

"Better a secret than have you blame yourself."

"Why did she have me in the first place if it made her
so sad?"

"Your mother . . . She was a complicated person."

"So I keep hearing."

"She could be very stubborn. I think she had you
because everyone was telling her not to go through with
it. She wanted to prove us all wrong."

"Us?" I said. "Did you tell her not to have me?"

Ruby leaned against the doorframe and sighed. "I
didn't know you then."

"Who has a child to prove a point?" I asked.

"What Melody never realized is that if you always do
the opposite of everyone else, you end up being just as
restricted as if you always do what you're told. You end up
feeling every bit as trapped."

"Is that how she felt? Trapped by me?"

"She was trapped by her decisions. Not by you, lad."

CHAPTER 33

THE ETA

PATRICK CORNISH WAS THE FIRST MURDERER LIPHOOK
had ever interviewed.

"Mr. Cornish," said Liphook. "Do you understand
where you are?"

He wore the look of a man who had just woken up from
a terrible nightmare. "I'm in the hospital," he said at last.
"What's wrong with me?"

"I'm not a doctor. I'm a police officer," she replied.

"What's happened?"

"What do you remember about today?"

"The last thing I remember was tidying up after class
and then . . . Eddie was waiting for me outside. I'd offered
him a lift. Then I don't know what."

"It's Saturday today. There's no school."

"Saturday? No. This is Thursday I'm talking about."

"Perhaps it will help if I tell you what I know. This

morning, Saturday morning, you drove to the residence of David Maguire."

"I don't know who that is."

"You parked outside his farmhouse, found his gun, and shot him dead."

Cornish stared at her in utter disbelief. "There's been a mistake."

It was hard to believe she was talking to a murderer. "You then shot two children."

"I can't have. I've never . . . I wouldn't."

"The detectives will take a full statement from you when they arrive," said Liphook. "You can tell me anything. Why did you shoot the kids, Patrick?"

"I didn't. I wouldn't. Hold on, shouldn't I have a lawyer here?"

"You most definitely should, but it won't do you any harm to tell me what happened."

The door opened. Liphook turned, expecting to see a doctor or a nurse, but two men dressed in smart dark suits entered.

"Officer Liphook," said the taller of the two men. "Good job. First on the scene of the crime."

"You can't start like that," said the other. "You have to say who you are first."

"Officer Liphook," said the first. "My colleague and I are from a government agency affiliated with the Criminal Investigation Department."

"What agency?"

"It's called the ETA."

"What's that stand for?"

"We can't say," said the shorter man. "Why were you at David Maguire's today?"

"I followed a stolen car there, but this is the man you should be talking to," began Liphook.

"Yes, we are well aware of Mr. Cornish's involvement, thank you," said the first.

"My involvement?" said Cornish. "What's going on? Who are you people?"

"Please, Mr. Cornish, all will be made quite clear to you in due course," said the first man.

"Actually . . ." said the other. The two men turned around and whispered quietly to each other, then turned back to face Liphook and Cornish. "Sorry. My colleague has pointed out that it will not be made clear to you, but that can't be helped, so let's move on, shall we?"

"What?" exclaimed Cornish.

"Now, Officer Liphook, tell us about this stolen car."

"It belongs to Mrs. Spinks. Her cat was in the back. She reported it stolen."

"The cat or the car?" asked the shorter man.

"Both. I spotted the car driving erratically along the main valley road, so I followed it to a field, where two juveniles abandoned it. I then followed them to the farmhouse."

The taller of the two men made a note of this in a pad, then flipped over the page and showed it to his colleague. "Yes, that seems about right. Did you apprehend the car thieves?"

"They're in the hospital. Their names are Lauren Bliss and Eddie Dane."

"Eddie stole a car?" said Cornish.

"Lauren Bliss?" From their reaction, the two clearly knew the name. "Where is she now?"

"In the hospital bed," said Liphook. "But I think you're missing the point. The gun was fired by Patrick Cornish. He killed a man and shot two kids."

The two men weren't listening. They turned to leave.

"What about me?" asked Cornish.

"Well, you probably want to use loss of memory as your defense," said the shorter man.

"Yes. Good luck with that," said the other.

"What? This isn't right," protested Cornish.

"You've only yourself to blame," said the taller man.

"In a sense," added the shorter one.

"In a sense," repeated the other.

"What's going on?" demanded Liphook. "I want to see your credentials. Who are you people?"

Neither man answered, and she followed them along the corridor to the bed where Lauren Bliss had been—only to find it empty. Lauren was gone. In the bed next to hers lay Eddie, still unconscious. Ruby was sitting next to him, with her head slumped over the side of the bed, fast asleep.

"None of this makes any sense," said Liphook.

"Yes," said the taller man. "I'm afraid that is correct."

CHAPTER 34

SECOND SATURDAY

MY SECOND SATURDAY MORNING, I SAT AT THE KITCHEN table, watching the rain trickle down the window, wondering if each droplet was following the exact zigzagged line as before. I thought about Maguire's diagram explaining what would happen if you went back in time, and how it meant there would be two realities, each a copy of the other. How exact did it have to be? Was every droplet of water acting in the same way as the last time this all happened?

I was so entranced by the rain on the windowpane that I almost jumped out of my skin when the phone rang. I paused before answering. Ruby's friends knew not to call so early, which meant that it was Angus, but I wasn't in the mood to talk to him about trees.

"Eddie, lad, are you up? That's the phone," I heard Ruby shout from upstairs.

"I've got it," I responded. I picked up the receiver, but before I could say a word, I heard Maguire's voice say, "Eddie? Is that you? I understand now. You were right."

"What's happened? What do you understand?" I replied.

"I see now. You were right. It is possible to travel back. Come quickly. We must try to understand what happened to you."

"Why?"

"Because I think it may be extremely important."

"You didn't even believe me before," I said. "What's changed?"

"I've changed, Eddie," he said. "I've been back too."

"Where?"

"It's not important where I went. The question is where have you come from?"

"I'll come now," I said.

I grabbed my coat and shouted, "I'm going out." I don't know if Ruby heard, and I wasn't going to hang around waiting for her to respond.

This time, instead of trying to cross the muddy field, I continued down the hill until I found a lower path that brought me level with the farmhouse. I leaned my bike against the wall and knocked loudly on the door. The reply came not in the form of a voice, but as a gunshot.

A bullet ripped a hole in the door. I dived to the ground, facedown in the mud.

"That was a warning," yelled Maguire from the other side.

"Don't shoot! It's me, Eddie."

"Eddie who?"

"Eddie Dane. I was here yesterday."

"If you're from the agency, you have to declare it now. That's the protocol."

"I don't know what that means," I said.

Maguire opened the door. As usual, it got stuck halfway. "Blasted thing," he said, yanking it open. He was wearing the same white lab coat as before, but his eyes looked wild and frightened, and he had a graze on his head. "Why are you here?" he demanded.

"You called me," I said, still on the ground in the mud and the rain.

"When did I call you?"

"I don't know, fifteen minutes ago?"

"Why?"

"Why what?"

"Why did I call you?" he demanded.

"You said you knew what was going on and that you believed me about the jumping-back-in-time thing."

"Who's gone back in time?"

"Me."

"Ha," he said, waving the shotgun in my face. "So, you *are* echo jumping. I knew it. What's your originating version and time?"

"What are you talking about?"

"How far back have you jumped? What point in the future are you from?"

"Not really any point in the future. I only got as far as today, except it was different," I said, "and I don't know why it happened."

"You don't know?" he said. Then, after a moment's reflection, he repeated it. "You don't know." His eyes widened and he looked around, as though checking if anyone was there and said, with certainty this time, "You don't know. Yes. Inside now. It's not safe out here."

"Not safe? You're pointing a gun at me."

"Inside," snarled Maguire.

CHAPTER 35

ECHO JUMPING

I COULDN'T PUT MY FINGER ON HOW MAGUIRE WAS DIF-ferent, but he had definitely changed. It was more than the wild look in his eyes and the way his shaking hands gripped the gun. It was something about the way he moved as he flitted around the room, ensuring that the curtains were all drawn.

"You said I called you. How did I sound?" he asked.

"Excited, I suppose," I replied, "but why are you asking this like you don't know?"

"Never mind that. What did I say? What were my exact words?"

"You said that you had . . ." It was strange. As I tried to recall it, I realized I couldn't remember what he had said to me. A nagging thought occurred to me that it had never happened.

"It's hazy, isn't it?" said Maguire. "They're untethered

memories, shifting pasts. Classic early echo-jump side effects before I managed to fine-tune the process." He placed his hand to my temple. "Any hallucinations? Odd associations?"

"Yes."

"Tell me about the repeated days. What differences have there been?"

My first thought was of Scarlett, but I remembered her saying she would be in trouble if anyone discovered that I knew anything. I didn't want to mention her, but I did want to understand what all this was about. "My English teacher, Mr. Cornish, came here to kill you."

"Patrick Cornish?" he said.

"Yes."

"Interesting. Did he succeed?"

"In killing you?"

"Yes. In killing me."

"I think he did, yes. He used that gun. Or at least, I thought he did, only he can't have, can he?"

Maguire smiled. It was an odd reaction to being told that he had been shot dead. "Why were you here?"

"He was acting weird on my way home," I said, "so the next day I followed him and he came here."

"On your own?"

"On my own," I said.

"It would be in your best interests to tell me the truth.

Remember, I do have a gun." He held it up both as a reminder and a threat.

"It was just me," I said. "Now, will you tell me what's going on?"

"I very much doubt you could understand it."

"Try me."

"You are mid–echo jump. Since your originating point was here and you jumped back two days, I think we can safely assume that this, the first time particle accelerator, was used and that it was used in a hurry, meaning that whoever sent you back didn't have time to adjust the settings."

"What settings?"

"My first-ever jump was also back two days. Which leads us to the questions of who sent you back and why they didn't have time to adjust the settings. Who was here with you?"

"What's an echo jump?" I asked. "And how come you know all this when yesterday you didn't know anything? And how come you don't remember calling me? And why are you still pointing a gun at me?"

Maguire lowered the gun and placed it on the armchair.

"Maybe I should show you the recording."

"What recording?"

"People love the recording."

Maguire walked into the back room, where he picked up a camera and found a lead to connect it to one of the computers. After a little jiggling of wires and pressing buttons, an image came on-screen of Maguire sitting on the stool in front of the blank wall.

"Watch this now," said Maguire. "This is a real piece of history. Or at least, it will be."

CHAPTER 36

DEMONSTRATION

"MY NAME IS DAVID MAGUIRE, AND THIS IS A SCIENTIFIC demonstration."

The on-screen Maguire reached forward and clumsily swiveled the camera around to show the equipment that was pointing directly at him.

"I have, for some years now, believed that there exists a particle that governs our relationship with time. Those of my peers who doubted this belief should understand that I feel no ill will toward them. In fact, without their firm hands pushing me away from the established scientific community, I would never have been able to fully dedicate my time to this pursuit.

"Soon I will publish a paper detailing the specifics of my findings, but for the sake of this demonstration, try imagining that, just as a strand of DNA holds the blueprint of life, the time particle contains all information pertaining to that which has already occurred: the past. Whether it also contains that which is yet to occur, I do not know. But let's not try to run before we can walk. What I am sure of is that this particle governs our forward movement through time. Let us take this book as an example."

Maguire held up the hardback copy of *Frankenstein*.

"A book contains many traces of history. This is a story written by Mary Shelley in 1816, published in 1818, then again with changes by the author in 1831. This edition was published in"—Maguire opened it up and checked the date inside—"1937. I can't tell you how many owners it has had, how many hands have held it, or whose eyes have perused the words. What I can say is that each molecule that makes up each page is governed by time particles that ensure that this book travels forward through time. It began life in pristine condition, but now its pages have smudges from dirty fingers, folds from those who wanted to keep their place, and other marks, all common in old books. Time, as we have always understood it, allows for things to become worn, and we would all be very surprised if the book's condition improved over the years.

"I will now use this book to demonstrate how time is not what we thought it was. For some reason, best known to the publishers, there are two completely blank pages at the back." He held the book open to its back pages, first putting it too close to the camera, causing it to go out of focus, then moving it farther away before lowering it. "I have never read this book and only selected it because I was reminded of it recently. Now, watch carefully as I turn to a page, completely at random."

He flicked through the pages and chose one.

"I will now read the first sentence my eyes have fallen upon. *The different accidents of life are not so changeable as the feelings of human nature.*"

He paused to reflect on this before continuing.

"That is the first time I have read that line. It's rather good and oddly appropriate. Watch now, as I turn on the time particle accelerator, which will send me on a short jump back along my own timeline. This past is encoded in the particles that govern my existence, so you will not be able to join me on this journey. Instead, you will witness me falling into a short temporal coma. Please do not be alarmed by this."

He leaned forward and flicked a switch, then sat back in the chair.

"My time perception is now being . . ."

His voice drifted away and he fell forward, crashing straight into the camera, and for a few seconds the screen showed nothing but the ceiling, until Maguire picked up the camera. This time he had a graze on his temple.

"Now look," he said.

He pointed the camera at the book, opened it, and

revealed on the blank pages, written in messy handwriting, this sentence: *The different accidents of life are not so change-able as the feelings of human nature.*

He swung the camera back to his face. "Obviously, you're thinking this is a trick. That I could have written this while the camera was not pointing at me. But I assure you it is not. The acceleration of my governing time parti-cles sent me back into my own past. Physically I remained here, but my conscious self returned to an earlier point in my life. It entered this very body two days ago. Thursday morning. I was not there long, just long enough to find a pen and write the sentence that I had just read. To avoid confusion, rather than labeling this time travel, which has too many connotations and inherent inaccuracies, I am calling this echo jumping because I returned to an earlier point of my existence, just as a sound wave can bounce back in the form of an echo. I have yet to fully establish the consequences of causality involved in this temporal shift, but as you've seen from my demonstration, it is possible to alter events. Whatever the truth, this is a significant leap forward, both in the history of science and in the science of history."

CHAPTER 37

AN ALTERED VERSION

MAGUIRE PRESSED STOP ON THE CAMERA. "ANY QUES-tions?"

I had so many I didn't know where to begin. He dis-connected the camera, but the image of his frozen face remained on the monitor.

"Go on," he said. "You can ask me anything. This is a museum, after all. Or it will be. I believe they call this one the Discovery Room."

"Okay," I said, "if you went back in time and wrote the sentence two days ago, then why wasn't it there when you opened up the book in the first place?"

"That is a very good question, and one that will take many years of research and speculation to answer." He switched off the monitor.

"Which is another way of saying that you don't know," I said.

Maguire smiled patiently at me. "I did not say it was unanswerable. I said it would take time, and indeed it did."

"I don't understand."

"You think I am the same man you spoke to this morning on the phone?"

"Aren't you?"

"Yes and no. This is certainly the same hand that dialed the number and called you." He wiggled his fingers. "I am speaking with the same vocal cords that spoke to you. But this is not the same consciousness." He tapped his forehead. "In my timeline, I have never called you on the phone. Not that I can remember anyway."

"But . . . I . . . What?"

"I have jumped back to this point from a version of the future."

"You're from the future?"

He nodded. "We don't have time to go into my reasons for being here, but it does mean that I can answer your question about the outcome of the experiment, although I don't hold a great deal of hope you'll fully understand this first time. It takes the world a long time to adjust to the complexities of echo technology. A long time indeed."

"Echo technology?"

"Don't get too distracted by the technical terms. Think about it this way: there are two predictable consequences of the experiment with the book. In the first, it simply doesn't work. In the second, it does. We call these two possibilities the originating and the altered versions. In the originating version, I am disappointed by the failure yet intrigued by the inability to affect the future. In the altered version, or the echo, the experiment is a success. The words have miraculously appeared on the page."

"Then how come they weren't there when you opened the book?"

"Intriguing, isn't it? Imagine you're a bungee jumper leaping off a bridge over a river. At the farthest point of the jump, you dip your hand into the water and pick up a stone from the riverbed. The cord then snaps back and returns you to your jump point with the stone in your hand."

"Bungee jumping?"

"Yes, except that the bridge in this case is your originating point in time, the river is the past, and the stone is whatever you changed when you went back."

"There's a bit of difference between taking a stone out of a river and changing the past."

"Not as much as you might think. The river's flow is altered, much as the course of events are changed. These analogies are never perfect. Echo technology is extremely complicated even when simplified. The important thing is that it is possible to go back to the past and affect a future. But here is the thing that most struggle with: while the bungee rope itself remains intact, each jump has both out-comes. Both the originating and altered versions coexist."

"How do you know?"

"Try repeating the experiment with the book, and you soon discover that you have a fifty-fifty success rate, because half the time you'll return to the originating version, not the altered version."

"So, which is the real one?"

"*Real* is not a helpful word. Time doesn't distinguish between versions."

"You're saying that every time you do this thing with the book, you're making another version of the world."

"That's a very neat way of putting it. As I continue with my investigations, I will discover how the jump cord can be broken, once a return is made to the originating version, to destroy the altered version. This prevents all that messing-about-with-the-past business and makes it possible to echo jump back and do whatever you like without worrying about what your actions will do to the future."

"But if you'd done that, then the thing with the book wouldn't have worked."

"Exactly. I performed these early jumps before I learned how to clean up these versions."

"And before it was the law to do so."

We both turned to see Scarlett standing in the doorway.

The curly red hair was gone. In its place was straight blond hair. The green-blue eyes were the same, though.

"Hi, Eddie," she said.

"Scarlett?"

"Lauren," said Maguire. "I should have guessed."

"Lauren?" I said.

"Hello, David," she replied. "Don't worry about names, Eddie. Please let me handle this—and no heroics this time."

"I didn't let him know there was anything to know," I said.

"That's right," said Maguire. "Eddie has been acting convincingly ignorant since he arrived, almost like someone who didn't have the faintest idea of what's happening to him. There are protocols about that."

"I'm not here to talk procedure," said Scarlett. "I'm here to take you in. It's time, David. The trial is under way."

"A trial in which I'm accused of a murder," he said.

"Murder?" I said. "No. Cornish shoots *him.*"

"Patrick Cornish is a footnote in all this," said Maguire. "His group of anti-echo activists thought they could change things using the technology they were trying to get rid of."

"He's right," said Scarlett. "Cornish has already stood trial for his actions here. This is much more important than that. It's time to tidy up."

"Tidying up? Is that what they call it these days? What

if I prefer it messy like this?" Maguire picked up the gun and pointed it at her.

"Hey, no!" I exclaimed. "Scarlett's protecting you. Tell him you're here to protect him."

Maguire was looking at her, not me. "Is that right, Scarlett? Are you here to protect me?"

"I'm here to do my job," she replied.

"No matter the consequences?" he said.

"It's the law. You know that. Now, tell me where to find you and let's resolve this."

Maguire took a side step, keeping the gun leveled at Scarlett. "Why did you send your boyfriend echo jumping?" he asked.

"I'm not her boyfriend," I said. "I mean, I don't think . . . That's not to say . . ."

"He's not important," replied Scarlett.

I tried to hide my disappointment.

"He said he was shot," said Maguire. "Don't say you broke protocol to save his life?"

"Yes. That's what happened."

Maguire eyed her suspiciously. "No, that's not it, is it? There's no sentimentalism here. Oh, I see . . . He's your witness."

Maguire pointed the gun at me.

"Don't make matters any worse," said Scarlett.

"I'll break this jump cord and end this version anyway," said Maguire. "It makes no difference."

"You know that doesn't excuse your actions. It'd be easier for everyone and better for you to come quietly."

"Sorry, Lauren," said Maguire. "I need a little more
time."

Maguire pulled the trigger.

The gun was still pointing at me.

38

THE RESILIENCE OF RUBY DANE

LIPHOOK HAD ADMIRED THE WAY RUBY DANE HELD IT together even when the doctor explained to her the seriousness of her grandson's condition. After the doctor had left, Liphook stayed with Ruby. She didn't want to add to her stress so she gave her several opportunities to change the subject, but Ruby didn't seem to mind going over the details.

"So, Eddie was supposed to be tree-climbing with his friend Angus . . ." Liphook checked her notes. "Angus Sandling."

"Yes, Angus came around to call for him this morning, but we both assumed that Eddie must have got mixed up and gone to his house."

"And David Maguire . . . You knew that he was living nearby and that he might be Eddie's father. Is that right?" asked Liphook.

"I honestly assumed he had moved."

"Why?"

"I don't know. I never saw him around."

"Had he never tried to make contact with Eddie?"

"No. I don't think he ever wanted anything to do with the boy. He came around once after Eddie's mother died, but that was it. I think he was relieved to be turned away."

"So, he did try to be a part of the boy's life at one stage?"

"I wouldn't call it trying. He offered."

Liphook snapped her notebook shut. "Presumably Maguire changed his mind and got in contact with him."

"I suppose so."

"You said you didn't know the girl Eddie was with. What about the teacher, Mr. Cornish? How well did Eddie know him?"

"He used to give him a lift home sometimes. I think Eddie looked up to him."

"Like a father figure?"

"You're asking all these questions," said Ruby, "and I'm doing my best to answer them, but does any of this stuff make sense to you?"

"Not yet," said Liphook.

The silence that followed was broken when the swing doors at the end of the corridor burst open and a gaggle of medics charged in with a boy lying on a stretcher. Both his legs were badly cut. As they passed, Liphook sharply drew in her breath at the sight of the exposed bones and torn flesh. From the fast-talking medics, she picked out the words "suspected concussion," "both legs broken," "damaged vertebrae," and "potential hypothermia."

They disappeared as quickly as they had arrived and Liphook turned to Ruby, to find that the color had drained from her face.

"That was him," said Ruby.

"Who?"

"That was Angus. That was Eddie's best friend. He must have gone climbing without him and fallen."

Liphook could hear the confusion and fear in Ruby's voice. She wished there was something she could do to help. Something she could do to make sense of it. There was nothing.

39

THIRD THURSDAY

I SHUT MY EYES IN AGONY AS THE BULLET TORE through my body, but the pain vanished as though it had never been there. I staggered back but my head hit something hard. The collision brought new pain. I opened my eyes and found I was no longer in the farmhouse. I was outside, under the bus shelter in the pouring rain. My clothes were wet. I tapped my schoolbag but my copy of *Frankenstein* was gone. The bus arrived with a splash in the puddle.

"Ready, Eddie?" began Bill. "Then hold on steady—"

"I'm back here again?" I said.

"Yep," said Bill, "and if you're wanting the school, you're in luck because that's—"

"The only place you go," I interrupted.

I could see Angus wiping away the condensation on the window to see out.

"Come on, Eddie," said Bill. "I can't wait around all day. We've got places to go."

"Not this time," I said. "I need answers."

I turned and ran. Bill shouted after me, but his words were lost among the shifting memories in my head, each of which wriggled and writhed whenever I tried to see it clearly. In this storm of confusion, I heard the line "*A monotonous yet ever-changing scene.*" I knew it was from *Frankenstein* but had no idea what it meant or why I had remembered it. It felt like a memory someone else had left behind.

I grabbed my bike from the shed and spotted Ruby's silhouette behind the frosted glass of the bathroom window. There was no point talking to her. She had lied to me my whole life.

I rode my bike hard up the hills and allowed it to go so fast down slopes that I almost lost control. I approached Maguire's farmhouse from the lower road but slowed down as I got nearer. Something was different. There was an old brown car parked outside.

I leaned my bike against a wall and walked to the front door. This time I knocked and quickly stepped to the side, just in case, having no desire to be shot at again.

"One second," said Maguire. He opened the door and I kicked it hard to get it past the floorboard. It swung open, taking him by surprise, and sent him staggering back into the room. Had the piles of books been there, he would have knocked them over, but they were gone. He glared at me angrily. "Eddie? What are you doing here?"

"Which one are you, then?" I said.

"Missed the bus again, did you?" he said. "Well, come on." He grabbed a set of keys from a bowl by the door and stepped out, pulling the door shut behind him.

"I . . . What?"

"Otherwise you'll be late."

I followed him to his car. He got in and I was clearly expected to do the same.

"But . . . You know me?"

"Sorry, you know I don't really understand your jokes, Eddie. Buckle up."

I got in and pulled the seat belt on. Maguire had to yank his several times before he could click it into place. "I thought it was your mother when you knocked. We have a busy day ahead of us."

"My . . . my mother?"

"We're almost ready for human testing, can you believe it? Tomorrow, I think. A few more wrinkles to iron out."

"My mother?" I repeated.

"The rodents have responded quite well so far. I mean, except for the deaths, of course."

"You said *my mother.*"

"Are you all right?" said Maguire. "You appear to be stuck in a loop."

"In a loop?"

"You're repeating yourself."

"My mother's alive?"

"Ha! Still in bed, was she? Dead to the world? We were working late last night, I suppose."

"If she's alive, I want to go home," I said. "I want to see her."

"You're already late for school. It's better if I drop you there, then pick her up on the way back."

Maguire turned on the radio. A crackly voice was talking about something or other, but all I could hear was the buzzing of my brain as I tried to come to terms with what was happening to me. Had I somehow landed in a version of the world in which I had a mother? If so, I needed to see her, but what could I do? Jump out of the car?

For a moment, I considered jumping out of the car.

"I can't go to school today. I don't feel well," I said.

"Interesting."

"Yes. I keep going back in time, except things are different each time and now Melody has come back to life and I need to find out what's going on and not spend the day listening to the same lessons for the third time in a row."

Maguire nodded. "That sounds about right."

"You believe me?" I said.

"Sorry, Eddie, I was listening to the radio. Did you hear that? They just said we're heading for the wettest month since records began. Not hard to believe. Seems like it's been raining for weeks."

CHAPTER 40

THE MIDDLE OF NOWHERE

MAGUIRE WAITED AND WATCHED ME FROM HIS CAR, making sure I walked all the way up to the school building. Once inside, I was stuck on the slow-moving conveyor belt of that school day. Short of running out the front door, there was no way off it. I signed the late register, then went into assembly. Mr. Cornish sat by the side of the hall. PC Liphook stood at the front, speaking to Mrs. Lewis. My class was already sitting down, so I had to push my way along the row to get to Angus.

"Where have you been?" he asked when I sat down.

"I have no idea," I replied honestly.

"I saw you at the bus stop. You ran off."

"How can everything be just the same?" I said. "I mean, if so much is different, then how can all this be the same? I don't see how it can."

"It is confusing," agreed Angus.

"Wait. Do you know what I'm talking about?" I said.

Angus laughed. "No, but I agree that what you're saying is confusing."

Mrs. Lewis stood up. "Now, everyone, we have a very special guest, so let's show her what a polite and well-behaved school we are as we welcome Officer Liphook."

The usual round of applause followed.

"Community," began Officer Liphook. "Who can tell me what that word means?"

Something inside of me snapped.

"Oh, come on." I didn't bother raising my hand. "It means looking out for each other, being selfless, and sticking to the rules," I shouted.

Mrs. Lewis was on her feet, scowling at me, but I didn't care.

"Well, yes, that's right," said PC Liphook, looking a little thrown by the interruption.

"Good," I said. "Now can we move on to the bit where everyone asks about guns."

"Edward Dane!" yelled Mrs. Lewis.

"Well, look at her. She's as bored as I am and this is her first time around. And do you know why she's bored? Because this valley where we live is nowhere. Actually, no. It's worse than that. It's the middle of nowhere. Do you know why people come here on holiday? It's because they want to get away from it all, and you can't get away from everything unless you're visiting somewhere where there isn't anything—and that must be nowhere."

"Enough!" shouted Mrs. Lewis.

"I don't care. None of this matters," I said.

I could see Cornish looking concerned. I glanced at Angus, smiling nervously. None of them seemed real to me. I felt dizzy. The voices were back.

"*There's no medical reason for him to be in this state*," said one.

"*Eddie, can you hear me?*" said Ruby.

"*Can you help? I'm lost*," said a third voice. *Scarlett*, I thought. It was Scarlett's voice, but none of them remained, and the next one I heard belonged to Mrs. Lewis.

"My office, Eddie, please."

I nodded and made my way out of the hall, feeling the weight of everyone's eyes upon me.

Mrs. Lewis turned to PC Liphook. "Sorry, Officer Liphook, you appear to be the unlucky recipient of one of Eddie's jokes. Please, do carry on."

"Thank you," she said. "So, what does community policing involve? How do the police help maintain a stable society?"

PC Liphook continued, but I was no longer listening.

I had heard it all before.

CHAPTER 41

ASK YOURSELF WHO'S LAUGHING

SITTING IN MRS. LEWIS'S OFFICE, I COULD HEAR THE scraping of chairs and thundering of feet as the assembly came to an end. I was thinking that if these events could happen over and over, exactly the same, then these students and teachers had no choice but to behave as they did. The chattering and clattering were meaningless. None of us really had a choice but to cling on to the swinging branch. I wished I could be so ignorant, but it was different for me. I understood that the world wasn't as it seemed. I had never felt so alone.

Mrs. Lewis entered the room and sat down behind her desk. "Is everything all right, Eddie?" she asked.

"I have no idea," I answered honestly. "Is this normal? For me, I mean. I don't even know what I'm like here."

"Since you ask," she said, "I would say you are a bright boy with a very individual sense of humor, but you need to understand when it is appropriate to make jokes and when it is not."

"Maybe you should call my mother?" I said.

Mrs. Lewis bit her lower lip. "I don't think there will be any need for that. Perhaps there's something you want to talk about."

"I don't think I could explain it to you."

"Try me. Maybe I'll understand."

"Nothing that's happening makes any sense." I heard my voice break and I blinked back my tears.

"This is about your mother, isn't it?" Mrs. Lewis picked a pen off her desk and placed it carefully into a pot. "I know she and your grandmother have been arguing a lot recently, but you mustn't worry on behalf of other people."

"How do you know that they're arguing?"

"Mr. Cornish mentioned it," she said. "It's good you feel you can open up to him about these things, but I'd like to think you can speak to me about them too. I'm trying to help here, but you need to understand that your behavior this morning was totally unacceptable."

"I understand that. I'm sorry, Mrs. Lewis."

"And do you have an explanation?"

"It's like you said. It was a stupid joke."

"Yes, well, the thing about jokes is that you have to ask yourself who's laughing."

"Yes, Mrs. Lewis."

After Mrs. Lewis let me out, I went straight to my classes,

so I didn't get a chance to speak to Angus properly until lunchtime.

"These meatballs are amazing," he said, taking a bite. "I mean, you forget how good they are."

"Angus, we have them every Thursday," I said.

"Six days is a long time without meatballs, Eddie."

I knew Angus was trying to make me laugh because he was worried about me, but it annoyed me when he asked, "How are you?"

"Don't you start," I replied.

"Start what?"

"This asking *How are you?* and looking-worried business. Everyone wants to know how I am. I don't even know myself."

"I can help you with that. You're Eddie Dane."

"Who's he?" I asked, because I no longer knew.

"Here, at this point in time, he's my best friend," said Angus.

It struck me as odd that he hadn't brought up my behavior in assembly, when half the school was looking at me like I was crackers. I put it down to Angus not wanting to cause me any more embarrassment than I had already caused myself. Whatever the reason, I was grateful for it.

42

QUESTIONS AND ANSWERS

"I WANT US TO NAME AS MANY MONSTERS AS WE CAN, comrades."

Cornish's repeated words were nothing to the crackling and spitting questions in my head, but I was dragged into the present by a new response from Angus.

"Frankenstein," he called out.

Angus had been acting strangely all afternoon. He had seemed more engaged with the lessons and kept jiggling his legs under the table.

"You mean Frankenstein's monster," replied Cornish.

"No. I mean Victor Frankenstein, the man," said Angus. "It seems to me the monster only becomes a monster when his creator rejects him. Before that, it's innocent, isn't it? Frankenstein is the real monster."

It was rare to see Cornish lost for words, but he was

clearly thrown by this. "Impressive," he said. "Have you actually read the book, Angus?"

"No, but I saw a really good film of it once," he replied.

"That's great, but in a film the story has already been interpreted numerous times. The screenwriter, director, actors, and all the countless others who made that film gave their interpretations. With a book, the reader must do all that him—or her—self." Cornish grabbed the pile of books from the desk and began distributing them among the class. As usual, the same copy with the yellow-faced man landed on my desk.

"So, can anyone tell me this book's alternative title?"

By now, I had learned to drift off at the first sign of repetition. I stared at the book. The man in the picture stared back with his dark eyes. All this time I had thought of him as old, but now that I looked, I saw that the lines on his forehead were the product of a frown rather than of age. Under that beard was a man no older than Cornish. I opened the book and flicked through it, looking for the sentence that had popped into my head with such determined clarity. I failed to find it, then realized I could no longer remember it. Instead I turned to the final page of the book and read the last line:

He was soon borne away by the waves, and lost in darkness and distance.

Lost in darkness and distance. I liked the sound of that. It was how I felt. The more I thought about it, the more I realized it was how I had always felt. I turned the page to the appendix and some more notes and ads for other books. Finally I got to the last page.

Any questions?

It was spidery writing with a circle over the *i*. I don't know how, but I knew it was aimed at me. Any questions? I had more questions than I knew what to do with. I picked up a pen and wrote:

What is going on?

I closed the book and looked around. Everyone was listening to Cornish reading *Frankenstein.* I opened my copy again and saw that another sentence was written below mine.

You'll need to be more specific.

My astonishment that this sentence had miraculously appeared on the page was tempered by my annoyance at the reply. I stared at it. I felt like throwing the book across the room. Instead I wrote:

What question should I ask?

This time when I shut the book I caught Angus's eye. I waited until he looked away before opening the book again.

What is the truth about Melody Dane's death?

I picked up the pen to write again, but this time Cornish spotted me. "Eddie Dane!" he yelled. "Are you writing in that book?"

"No, sir," I said, quickly closing it.

"I'm glad to hear it. I've managed to beg, borrow, and steal enough copies for you each to have one, but I will want the books back, so please treat them with respect. Now, let's see how Mary Shelley begins her masterpiece, shall we?"

CHAPTER 43

WHICH YOU ARE YOU?

CORNISH WAS BACK ON SCRIPT. "I'M GOING STRAIGHT off tonight, Eddie, if you want a lift home."

"Thanks."

"How about you, Angus?"

"Er . . ." Angus looked at me, unsure what the right response was.

"His mum is picking him up," I said.

"That's right," he said. "Honestly. I'd forget my own . . . you know, if it wasn't something or other."

Cornish grinned. "Just you and me, then, Eddie. I'll see you by the car once I'm done here."

I followed Angus out into the corridor with the rest of the class.

"How come you forgot about your mum coming to pick you up?" I asked.

"Slipped my mind," he said.

"You don't usually forget."

"Maybe I was distracted by whatever you were writing in the book."

We stopped and looked at each other, each suspicious of the other, neither of us knowing what to say next.

"Did anyone write back?" asked Angus.

The last of my classmates had gone now, meaning it was just the two of us in the corridor.

"You know?" I said.

"Eddie?" he replied. "I mean, *Eddie*?"

"Yes?"

Angus lowered his voice. "Are you Eddie from now or from, you know, my now?"

"When's your now?"

"I'm not supposed to say. What about you? When's your now?"

"Kind of now, but not here now."

"Hold on—if you don't know what now I'm from, then you're not from my now and we shouldn't be talking."

We stepped out into the car park, and I wondered if it was possible to feel any more confused. Cornish had traveled back in time to kill Maguire. Scarlett had traveled back to stop him and then a second time to arrest Maguire. What had Angus come back for, and how could I possibly trust him?

"Why are you here?"

"If you have to ask, I definitely can't tell you," he said.

"You're as bad as she is."

"Who?"

"I'm not supposed to say," I told him.

"Last call for anywhere but here," cried Bill.

Angus and I stared at each other, neither knowing what to say next.

"We shouldn't talk," said Angus.

"Why? Are you worried that we might say something that actually makes sense?"

Angus laughed. The car flashed its headlights outside the school gate.

"I guess that's me," said Angus. "I'll see you, Eddie."

He ran to the car.

I blew into my cupped hands and stamped my feet to keep warm, thinking about the future Cornish and how all that passion I had admired would one day make him a murderer.

"Hi, Eddie. Get in, then," said Cornish.

"Can I ask you something, sir?" I said, sitting in the passenger seat. "Does my mother ever come to pick me up?"

Cornish nodded as though to say that he understood what I was really asking. "Mrs. Lewis said she spoke to you. I hope you don't mind that I'd told her about our chat. She only wants to help. We all do."

"Yes, but does Melody ever come and pick me up?"

"Listen, Eddie, I know you're angry at your mother for being so busy all the time, and it's fine to express that anger."

"You're not answering my question," I protested.

"Often you'll find the answers we seek don't always match the questions we ask, but if you really want me to answer, then no, your mother doesn't have a car. You told me she had a scare once and hasn't driven since. Has this got something to do with what happened in assembly this morning?"

"No, sir."

Cornish turned on the radio but found only static and switched it off again.

"You know, lots of adults think the young don't have anything to worry about, because they don't have jobs or mortgages or money worries. But the worries you have at your age are worse than ours, because you feel powerless to do anything about them. Do you know what I mean by that?"

"I think so," I replied. Powerless was exactly how I felt.

"I'm a teacher because I want to make a difference to the world. Education is where change starts. My experience of school was that it was all about doing the right thing, following instructions, revising, and getting through exams."

"Doesn't sound all that different," I said.

He laughed. "You're right, but while I'm in a lesson like that one today and the ideas are flowing, the minds are thinking, and we're all embracing the chaos, I'm able to show how limitless imagination is. That's how you bring about real change in the world. You imagine it."

I didn't respond.

"The world is yours to change, Eddie, but if you want it to be a better place, if you want to stop the rich and powerful from exploiting everyone and everything this planet has to offer, you can't sit around waiting for others to do something. You need to take matters into your own hands."

I thought back to Maguire's lab, when Cornish had pointed the gun at my chest. When he stopped the car outside my house, I felt the seat belt tighten, reminding me of the pain of the bullet.

44

THE TRIAL

LIPHOOK HAD BEEN RETIRED FROM POLICE WORK FOR several years when the two men from the hospital turned up on her doorstep. After all this time, she should have been surprised to see them again, but deep down she had always expected them to return one day. She was alone when they arrived. She was often alone these days. She invited them in, and they sat down in her living room and explained that she had been summoned to a trial.

"A trial about what?" she asked.

"I'm afraid we aren't at liberty to say," said the taller man.

"Back then you said you were from the ETA," she said. "It's something to do with echo technology, isn't it? You were from the future."

"We're not at liberty to say," said the shorter man.

"No one knew anything about you," said Liphook, "but

I've had plenty of time to think about it. Is that what the trial's about? Is it about that night Maguire was murdered?"

"We can only tell you that you are being summoned as a witness." The tall man pulled out a small black device about the size of a mobile phone.

"Where do I have to go?"

"It's more a matter of when," said the shorter of the two.

"When, then?"

"We're not at liberty to say," replied the taller one. "Now, please look into this lens." He held up the device. Hoping it might provide answers to some of the questions that had plagued her over the years, Liphook looked into the lens. There was a flash of light, and she found herself in a large, brightly lit room crammed full of onlookers, officials, and journalists.

Patrick Cornish was standing in the dock. From the lines on his face, Liphook guessed it was around thirty years after that night at Maguire's farmhouse. Cornish looked like a man who had been given a long time to consider what he had done.

Lauren Bliss was there too. "Hello, Patrick," she said. "Do you understand why you are here today?"

"No, I don't. I've already stood trial for my crime. I've paid my debt."

"Agent Bliss, can we clarify the witness's meaning?" asked the judge, a keen-eyed man presiding over the trial.

"I have already been convicted for the murder of David Maguire," said Cornish.

Liphook looked over at David Maguire, who was also sitting in the room, very much alive. The whole thing was so bizarre.

"You killed Professor Maguire in the hope of preventing the discovery of echo technology," said Agent Bliss. "Is that correct?"

"That is correct. The Anti-Echo League believed that it was possible to travel back, terminate those responsible for its discovery, and stop it from ever being invented."

"Do you still think this was a feasible plan?"

"No. I understand now that this was not possible, but the failure of our methods does not negate the worth of our intention."

"What did you object to about echo technology?"

"You're using the wrong tense. I do object to echo technology."

Agent Bliss smiled. "Once an English teacher, always an English teacher."

"I'll tell you what I object to. Not the dangers of a split timeline, not the fragmentation of time. Mine is a moral objection. The Echo Corporation offers the world's richest people the opportunity to dip back into their pasts and relive their lives over and over, exploiting the world again and again. They don't have to worry about the world's future, hidden away in their own sordid pasts. Each time they travel back, they use their knowledge of the future for their own gain, exploiting the same people over and over. When it comes down to it, this technology is just another tool of repression."

"But the law now states that all jump cords must be broken, preventing echo jumps from being anything more than a brief, harmless diversion," said Agent Bliss.

"The rich will always find a way around laws that don't suit them. You don't even know how many versions there are out there created by this technology."

"That is precisely the question this trial is dealing with," said the judge.

"I don't believe this problem will go away while this technology is only affordable to the rich."

"Or those activist groups who break into echo chambers and perform illegal echo jumps," said Agent Bliss.

"The end justifies the means."

"I have a question," said the judge. "What if these rich that you so wholeheartedly disapprove of are going back to create better worlds? Do you still consider that abhorrent?"

Cornish smiled. "I know the rich too well."

He directed this comment to a woman who sat in a prominent position in the courtroom, next to a smartly dressed man who may as well have had the word *lawyer* printed on his head. This man stood up and said, "The

Echo Corporation believes it is in everyone's best interests to move on from this witness."

"I agree," said the judge. "He has already been convicted for his part. I fail to see his relevance here."

"His relevance here," said Agent Bliss, "is to help us ascertain precisely which versions are echoes. We must be certain that the version in which Professor Maguire was murdered by Patrick Cornish is an altered version and therefore subject to cleansing."

"Very well. Then who is our next witness?"

"The first police officer to arrive on the site of Maguire's murder. Angela Liphook," said Lauren Bliss.

Liphook took the stand and, over the next few hours, was questioned about the day at the farmhouse and hospital. Once everyone in the courtroom was satisfied with her story, the judge thanked her for her time and the court moved on to the next witness.

"Next, this court will hear the testimony of Melody Dane," said Lauren Bliss.

45

A LIFE WITH MELODY

WHEN I WAS LITTLE, I WOULD GET SO ANGRY ABOUT not having parents that I would stop breathing altogether. It was a long time ago, but I could still remember how all those awful feelings would drift away as I passed out. It was the only way I knew how to control it.

Now, here I was in a version of my life in which Melody had not died. But if she had never died, then this was no grand reunion. It was just an ordinary rainy Thursday afternoon. It was the strangest feeling ever.

Standing outside the door, key in hand, I heard her voice for the first time and was surprised at how real it sounded. And how angry.

"You could have burned the whole bloody house down, you batty old woman!"

I opened the door and saw a discarded pair of shoes

and coat in the hall. My mother stood in the doorway to the living room, her back to me.

"Don't be melodramatic," said Ruby, shielding her eyes from the light.

"You're calling me melodramatic? That's a joke." Melody spat the words at Ruby, who was lying listlessly on the sofa, half watching the quiz show.

I closed the door loudly but my mother did not turn. "Hello, darling," she said. "Have a guess what your grandmother did."

Darling, I thought. My mother called me *darling*. It sounded weird. No one had called me *darling* my whole life, and now here was a complete stranger saying it as though it meant nothing. "Go on, darling, guess," she said.

"She left the stove on?" I asked.

Finally, Melody turned. My first thought was that she looked older than her picture, which was stupid because of course she was older. "Yes," she said. "Your grandma will end up killing us all."

"She prefers *Ruby*," I said automatically.

"And I prefer not having to worry about being burned to the ground."

"She didn't mean to," I said.

"Trust you to side with her," said Melody.

What did that mean? Was I expected to dispute this, or was it true? My mother had suddenly materialized in my life as though she had always been there, and now I had to pick up clues about what she was like and who I was in this version of reality.

"And don't think you're off the hook either," she continued, sounding so very weary with anger. "David told me how you showed up at the lab this morning. You can't just expect him to give you a lift whenever you can't be bothered to get up in time for the bus."

"That's not what happened," I protested.

Melody put her hand to her temple and sighed. "Look, I know David and I have been working late a lot, but very soon this thing is going to change everything for us."

"Change everything how?" I asked.

"For a start, we won't have to live in this damp little hovel anymore."

"You mean my home?" asked Ruby.

"Yes," Melody replied. "This might be enough for you, but Eddie and I want something more, don't we, darling?"

"I . . . I don't know."

"Come on now, darling." Melody stroked my cheek. Her hand felt cold. "We'll have enough money to pay for someone to look after your grandmother."

"I don't want anyone," Ruby protested weakly.

"Oh, you'd rather die in a stupid accident and have me blame myself because you were too stubborn to admit you needed help."

"At least I'd get some peace if I was dead," said Ruby.

From her tone, I understood that this was a joke, but Melody didn't seem to see it like that.

"Impossible person," she muttered and stormed out.

Ruby turned back to the television. A contestant had just answered a question wrong, resulting in a klaxon sound. I went into the kitchen, where Melody was stomping back and forth, tidying up.

"That woman," she said. "I could throttle her sometimes."

I sat down at the table, watching this stranger in my house. She reminded me of a pigeon that had once flown into the kitchen and fluttered around, trying to find a way out until I opened the back door and released it.

"Sorry, darling," she said. "How was your day?"

"Oh, same old, same old," I replied. "How about you?"

"It was fine until I got back here," she said. "David and I are so close to our goal now. I know you don't understand the work we do, but I really think we're on the brink of something very exciting here."

"We're studying *Frankenstein* at school," I said. "Do you know it?"

"Yes. Mary Shelley," she said. "I've got a copy if you need one."

"It's about a scientist who messes with things he should leave alone," I said.

Melody located a wine bottle, opened it, then turned

to face me. "That's very funny," she said, "but David and I know what we're doing, darling. You'll understand soon enough."

From the way Melody plunked herself down at the kitchen table with a large glass of wine and pulled out a bundle of papers to read, I could tell it was up to me to cook. The cupboards were as badly stocked as ever, but I managed to pull enough ingredients together to make pasta. When it was ready, I took Ruby hers so she could eat on the sofa.

"Thanks, lad," she said.

"You know we would never leave you really," I said.

"You're a good egg," replied Ruby.

I went back to the kitchen and sat down to eat with Melody. She began eating without saying thank you. "Is she still moping?" she asked.

"It's just a down day. She'll be fine again tomorrow," I replied.

"You don't need to defend her, you know. She's old enough to answer for her own actions, as are you. Now, are you going to tell me what you were doing at David's this morning?"

"It was like you said. I missed the bus."

All my life, I had imagined what it would be like to sit down and eat dinner with my mother. Now that it was finally happening, I was sitting there telling lies. I desperately wanted to have all those conversations I had imagined having with my mother. I wanted to tell her how much I had missed her and ask her a million questions, but I didn't know where to start. I watched her eating the food I had cooked and gulping mouthfuls of wine, oblivious to my feelings. I felt angry with her. How could she not know that we had been parted all this time? How could she not understand what this moment meant to me?

"You shouldn't treat David like a father," said Melody.

"You mean, because he isn't?" I asked.

"I mean, because I'm your mother and I'm asking you not to."

"Do you really think you'll make money out of this time stuff?" I asked.

"A lot of money, darling," she said, her eyes burning with excitement. "We'll be able to have anything we want. We'll be able to do anything we want. Selling time is the same as selling power. It's something everyone wants."

CHAPTER **46**

DEATH AND IGNOMINY

I TRIED SEVERAL TIMES TO TALK TO MY MOTHER ABOUT our life together, but it was impossible. What question could I ask that would reveal the truth about our lives together? All I could do was pick up clues from the way she sat at the table, leaning over a document, pen in one hand, glass of wine in the other, grunting her responses to my questions.

Eventually I went up to my room, only to find a cluttered dressing table by the window and piles of books all over the place. It wasn't my room. I spotted a black hardback copy of *Frankenstein* and picked it up, feeling like an intruder in my own bedroom. I turned to the last page of the book, but it was blank. I put it back on top of a pile and left. What had been the spare room was my bedroom now. All my life it had been full of Ruby's art materials and other bits and pieces that had nowhere else to live. Now it had my stuff in it. I sat down on my bed and took out my copy of *Frankenstein*. I half expected the photograph to fall out, but that was another world. Another version. Here Melody wasn't an overexposed memory but a real, living person in our house. It was strange, then, that there still weren't any photos on display like in Angus's home.

I looked at the last sentence handwritten in the book, with that distinctive circle over the *i*.

What is the truth about Melody Dane's death?

I wrote, Who are you?

Then I closed the book and reopened it, but there was no response. I closed it again, waiting longer this time, but when I looked, it remained unchanged. I tried placing it on a shelf and counting to ten. Still nothing.

Where have you gone?

My question was left hanging.

Disappointed, I turned to chapter five. Reading the part where Frankenstein made the monster, I was surprised by how suddenly he turned on his creation. Was it possible to spend so long on something only to lose faith in it as soon as it was finished? I carried on flicking through the book, half reading, half thinking, until I found these words:

Could the daemon, who had (I did not for a minute doubt)
murdered my brother, also in his hellish sport have betrayed
the innocent to death and ignominy?

I had no idea what this meant. What brother? What
murder? I realized that, after all this time with the book,
I still hadn't actually read it. As I stared at the page, it felt
as though the question was directed at me. Cornish always
went on about books coming to life, but this was different.
I didn't know what *ignominy* meant, but I understood the
word *innocent* well enough. I had been innocent when
Melody had died. Had I also been betrayed?

There was a quiet knock at the door and Ruby appeared.
She wore a pained expression on her face, as though the
world's volume was turned up too loud today.

"I'm going to bed now, lad," she said.

"Tomorrow will be better," I replied.

"That's a good way to look at it."

"Is Melody still up?" I asked.

Ruby nodded.

"Ruby," I said, "is it always like this?"

"It won't always be," she replied.

"But, I mean, you, me, and Melody. Are we ever happy?"

Instead of answering me, she said, "Hang in there, lad.
I know it's not much of a life, but it's all we've got."

"Maybe we'll do better next time," I added.

CHAPTER 47

THE CENTER OF THE UNIVERSE

I WAS STRUGGLING TO TELL WHAT WAS A DREAM AND what was real, but when I heard the front door slam and saw the time on my bedside clock, I knew I was awake and that I had overslept. I got up and quickly dressed. I could hear Ruby snoring, but Melody's bedroom door was open. She had gone out. I wolfed down some breakfast and ran to the bus stop, getting there as the bus was arriving. For the first time, I dodged the splash.

"Ready, Eddie? Then jump on board and hold on steady, Eddie."

Angus was waiting in his usual seat.

"I've got a message for you," he said.

"Who from?"

"Take a look."

He pulled out his copy of *Frankenstein*, which had a green cover with the title printed in black. Why did everything have to be about this book? He turned to the back pages, where someone had written:

Warn me about her.

"What does that mean?" I asked.

"Don't you recognize the handwriting?" said Angus.

I looked again and understood, except that I didn't understand—because it was my handwriting. Or at least, I think it was. No, I knew it was. The more I thought about it, the more I could imagine my hand forming the letters, almost as if it was a memory of something that had not yet happened. "When did I write it?"

"You in the future traveled to the past and wrote it so the now you would know not to trust her."

"But I thought you said you weren't allowed to tell me anything," I said.

"Yes, but you just told me to warn you about her, didn't you?"

"Did I?"

"You will. *Warn me about her* is you saying I need to warn you."

"Warn me about who?"

"You know who. I don't know what name she's using here, but her real name is Lauren Bliss."

"Scarlett? Maguire called her Lauren. Is she here?" I asked, trying not to sound too excited.

"Apparently there's a good chance she will be soon, and when you see her you can't tell her about me. She can't know what I'm doing here."

"*I* don't know what you're doing here."

"The less you know, the better."

"Then I'll be fine. I don't know anything."

"You know more than you think you know, but don't let on that you know anything except the things you know she knows you know."

"Angus, have you heard yourself?"

Angus smiled. "I agree it sounds mental, but it's important."

Bill slammed his foot down on the brake, and the bus screeched to a halt.

"One of these days he's going to kill us," I said.

"Surprisingly not," replied Angus. "Why have we stopped here?" He wiped the condensation from the window to reveal Scarlett standing at the bus stop. Her hair was red again, and she was wearing the same yellow raincoat she had worn the first day we met. When the bus doors opened she got on.

"Wellcome Valley School?" said Bill.

"Yes, which is lucky because it's the only place you go," she responded.

Bill laughed at what he obviously considered to be a very good joke. "What's your name, then?"

"Scarlett White. Should I take a seat and hold on tight?"

"Not a word," Angus whispered urgently.

Scarlett took her seat in front of us, then turned around.

"Hi, Eddie," she said.

"Do you two know each other?" asked Angus.

"Yes, we met on holiday last summer," she replied. "Remember, Eddie? My parents rented a cottage down the road from you. I'd got lost on my way to the shop and you cycled past. I asked for directions, but I'd forgotten the name of the place where I was staying. It took us ages to find the right cottage."

"You never mentioned that," said Angus.

"You were on holiday in France," I said.

The lie came so easily that I felt almost as though I could smell the freshly cut summer grass as we crossed a field of sunflowers under the clear blue sky.

"So, what are you doing here now?" asked Angus. "Not still looking for your way home, are you?"

"We just moved here. Listen, Angus, do you mind if I have a word with Eddie in private?"

"How do you know my name?" asked Angus.

"You're Eddie's best friend," said Scarlett. "You can't spend very much time with him without hearing about you, but I really would like to talk to him alone."

"Don't mind me. You two obviously have a lot to discuss." Angus squeezed past me to find a seat farther down the bus. Scarlett slipped into my seat while I moved next to the window. She looked at me in a way that suggested it had been some time since our last meeting. I couldn't tell whether she was happy or sad to be back, but I knew how I felt.

"Why's your hair keep changing color?" I asked.

"After all that has happened, are you entirely happy with that as your question?" she said.

"Only, it was blond last time."

"All right. We can talk about hair if you like. My hair is blond. This is a wig. Happy now? Have you any more hair-related questions?"

"No." I tried not to show my disappointment. "Where have you been?"

"A lot of places and a lot of times," she replied. "Now, I take it Angus has told you he's mid–echo jump?"

"Er . . ."

"He told you not to tell me. That's fine. You don't have to say anything you don't want to."

"How did you know? Have you got a zappy time device that tells you where people are from?"

"No. Angus isn't a very good actor. Has he told you what he's doing here?"

"Of course not. Telling me what's going on is against everyone's rules," I said pointedly.

Scarlett put her hand on my arm. "I'm really sorry, Eddie. I never wanted to drag you into all this."

"Was it you who sent me back both times?"

"Yes, but you did keep getting shot. I used Maguire's

time particle accelerator to send you on an echo jump."

"How come you can tell me all this now?" I asked.

"Because things have changed since we first met."

"Why did you send me back?"

"I needed to preserve this version of you."

"Why?"

"I'm a senior echo time agent. I investigate crimes committed using echo technology. If a jump cord is left unbroken, it usually means that someone is doing something they shouldn't."

"What are you investigating now?"

"My investigations rarely involve one thing at a time. It's what makes it such an interesting job. By my calculations, this is the third time I've met this version of you, and each time I've been looking into something different."

"What?"

"I can't go into details, especially since these things tend to be connected and this is an ongoing investigation."

"So, what's it got to do with me?"

"What do you think it's got to do with you?"

"It's something to do with Melody." I pulled out my copy of *Frankenstein* and showed her the back pages. "You wrote this, didn't you?"

She examined it. "It looks like my writing," she said. "Those circles over the *i*'s are what I use to identify writing as my own, which means if it isn't me, it's someone pretending to be me. Either way, it's best not to put too much faith in stuff written in the backs of books. Far too unreliable. Too easily intercepted."

"Don't you know if it was you who wrote it?"

"I know I haven't written in that book yet, but I don't know what I'll do in the future."

"But . . . Hold on. Er . . ."

"Eddie, there's going to be a lot you don't understand. Some people would argue that simply the fact that we are now having this conversation increases the chance of me writing in that book. Personally, I think it makes it less likely, but it doesn't matter."

"Yes, but . . . What if . . . But . . ." I fumbled, trying to order my jumbled thoughts.

"Eddie, time is a complicated business. The general rule is that if your head isn't hurting, you're not thinking about it hard enough."

"I don't want any more riddles," I said.

"I know, and I'll answer your questions soon enough, but at this stage, you only need to know one thing, and that is that you shouldn't trust anyone."

"If that's true, how can I trust you saying that?" I said.

"You shouldn't, but nor should you trust Angus, no matter what he tells you. Also, while we're at it, I'd rather he didn't know that I know that he knows about me."

"I'm not sure I could explain it even if I wanted to."

The bus pulled into the school car park and Angus joined us.

"Have you two caught up on everything?" he asked cheerily.

"Everything we can catch up on," replied Scarlett.

"Well, another day in the center of the universe awaits," he said.

CHAPTER 48

HISTORY OF THE FUTURE

THE MORNING'S REPETITIONS WERE LIKE THE TICKING of a grandfather clock. Occasionally I noticed them, but mostly they blended into the background. Scarlett proved as popular as ever this time around, so at break time, it was just Angus and me. We stopped by the Picasso portraits.

"Does she know about me?" he asked. "She does, doesn't she? Well, don't let her know I know that she knows. Okay?"

"Angus," I cried, louder than I had intended. "Enough."

Angus looked up at the portraits and said, "I remember these. I remember laughing about them. It feels like a lifetime ago. It's funny the things that get stuck in your memory."

"I don't think we have the same memories," I said. "We're from different versions, aren't we?"

"I suppose."

"So, am I different where you're from?"

"Yes and no. You're not much different at this point, but you do change. I suppose we all do. It's weird, all this echo stuff. I mean, is there a version where we didn't laugh at these pictures? Maybe there's a version where they weren't painted, or where they were done as normal pictures."

"Maybe there's a version where we're not friends," I said.

We both stared at the portraits in silence for a moment, and then Angus said, "She works for Maguire. Lauren, Scarlett, whatever you call her, she works for him."

"The last time they were together, she was trying to arrest him."

"I swear to you, Eddie, it's true."

"She said she was investigating crimes."

"She works for the Echo Time Agency, which Maguire set up. She's here to make sure he gets away with it."

"Gets away with what?"

"Come on, Eddie. Think. How is it possible that there is one version in which Melody died and another in which she is alive? Maguire went back in time and killed your mother."

"How?"

"I don't fully understand it myself, but according to you in the future, he'll travel back to the past to kill her. Except, for me, it's all in the past. Well, it was before I came back here. Now it's in the future again."

"That makes no sense."

"I totally agree, but you're proof that it's true. You've grown up in a world in which Melody died."

"Why would he do it? Why would he kill her?"

"To create a second version of events in which he discovers echo technology all alone. He didn't like sharing the glory with your mum, I guess. That's why Scarlett is trying to control you. Right now—in the future right now, that is—there's this big trial to decide which version of events is the originating one and which is the echo. You're the witness that proves that Maguire is guilty."

"Me?"

"Yes, because the world you grew up in was created when he killed her."

"How can that be possible?" If Angus was telling the truth, then the world I knew was a lie created by a murder. My whole life was an echo. Maguire had said that the term *real* was unhelpful, but if Angus was telling the truth, my whole life had been unreal. I could feel myself drifting away.

"I'm only telling you what you told me to tell you," said Angus. "Later on tonight, Maguire and Melody will discover the truth about the time particle accelerator. Shortly after that, they'll go public. There's this experiment they put online with a book."

"I've seen it," I said. "Well, a version of it."

"It's not long before things get pretty crazy after that because, well, they've invented time travel, haven't they?"

"I thought they didn't call it time travel," I said.

"True, but people are going backward and forward through time, so it is time travel really, isn't it? Anyway, soon after this, Maguire and Melody go their separate ways. Maguire sets up a government agency so he can control everything, while Melody starts a private company called the Echo Corporation. That's when she and you start making some serious money."

"What does this company do?"

"It's a kind of travel agency, only it's a time-travel agency."

"Like a holiday company?"

"Basically, yes. The super-rich pay millions to take holidays in time. *Holidays of the future are a thing of the past.* That's the slogan. Apparently you came up with that. Because they break the jump cords after each echo jump, your customers can go back and dabble in the past without it affecting their futures."

"This is all about holidays?"

"No, Eddie, it's all about money and power. Maguire gets jealous of Melody's success, not to mention her money. His agency is always investigating what the Echo Corporation is up to."

"Why?"

"There's this story that you and Melody allow your richest customers to keep their jump cords unbroken, so they can go back and live their lives over again in other versions of reality—but really, he's just jealous."

"How do you know all this?"

"One day you ask me to this fancy restaurant and, over dinner, you tell me what Maguire's up to."

"Which is what?"

"He's gone back and killed Melody, and now he's intending to wipe away the timelines in which she exists. That way, the version where she dies will be the only version left. He's trying to wipe her off the timeline altogether."

"Can he do that?"

"He can once the rest of the world decides that the timeline is becoming too fragmented. The ETA launches an investigation into every remaining line to shut down all the altered versions, leaving only the original one, but Maguire is trying to control which one remains. And he wants it to be the one you started in, the one without Melody."

"And I told you all this?"

"Yes."

"Did I look like I understood it?"

Angus laughed.

"Why did I tell you?" I asked.

The bell rang to signify the end of break.

"I'll explain later. Come on, we'd better get to class."

Before I followed him down the corridor, I looked up

at one of the portraits, in which one of the students had painted himself with two faces pointing in different directions. I didn't recognize the face, but I understood the feeling.

49

CHIPS AGAIN

SCARLETT DIDN'T ASK PERMISSION TO SIT WITH ME THIS time. She simply placed her tray with a baked potato and cheese on the table and sat down.

"You had salad last time," I said.

"You're getting confused. That was Thursday. This is Friday. But yes, it is useful to vary what you do when reliving the same moment. It keeps you focused on which now is now."

I picked up a chip with my fork. "So, how many more times do I have to eat this chip before this is over? They weren't even that nice the first time around."

Scarlett stole one and bit into it. "Tastes all right to me. You were talking to Angus during the break. What did he tell you?"

"Why do you want to know? So you can tell me that everything he told me was a lie, then tell me a load of more stuff to give me an even bigger headache?"

"I'm not here to give you a headache," said Scarlett.

"He said Maguire's going to go back and kill Melody. Or he's already done it."

Scarlett said nothing.

"Is it true?"

"It's certainly one possibility."

"He also said that you work for him."

"There are elements of truth in that too."

"He said you're trying to help him."

"Maguire? No, not the way Angus means. I'm here to find out the truth, which, as you're learning, isn't always that easy."

"He said something about Maguire destroying other versions, but I didn't really understand how."

"I'd be surprised if Angus did. This is advanced stuff even thirty years from now, but it's called an echo detergent because it cleans up any messy unwanted timelines."

"Unwanted?"

"Not all jump cords are destroyed immediately. The detergents help us at the ETA get rid of those leftover ones."

"So, you are helping Maguire?"

"I'm doing my job. The decision has been made to tidy up all altered versions. There are concerns about the timeline being fragmented. It hasn't been proven that it's a problem, but no one wants to take any risks. Besides, people don't like the idea that there are all these different versions of themselves wandering around, capable of jumping into their timeline at any point."

"Did Maguire kill my mother?"

Scarlett sighed. "What do you think? Do you think Maguire's capable of murdering Melody and wiping any trace of her from history?"

"How would I know?"

"I didn't ask you what you knew. I asked you what you thought. They can teach you how to work out who's doing what to whom, but the best tool you've got in the field is your ability to read people. You've met three versions of Maguire now. Did any of them seem capable of killing?"

"He shot me," I said.

"That's true, but he knew that timeline would be destroyed anyway, so I'm not sure that counts. He also knew I would save you."

"Why?"

"Because he knows I need you."

Scarlett must have seen the look on my face, because she quickly added, "For the investigation."

"Which is what?"

"The first time we met, I was investigating the timeline in which Melody died when you were a baby."

"So you're from a version in which she's still alive?" I asked.

She nodded. "Where I'm from, Melody Dane is one of the most powerful people in the world."

"Do you and I know each other in your version?" I asked hopefully.

"Yes, Eddie," she said patiently. "We know each other. That's why I had to make certain alterations to your time-line before I stepped onto that bus to investigate."

"What alterations?"

"I changed how we met. But then Cornish echo jumped into that line and complicated things even more."

"You mean when he traveled back to kill Maguire?" I said.

She nodded. "He appeared in the timeline that Thursday before midterm break, after the last lesson. He was expecting to kill Melody, but his jump got misdirected and he ended up in a version where she was already dead. When I got hold of him, I made sure he was returned to his originating point, where he was convicted for the murder. He's served his sentence now."

"But you only arrested him a few days ago."

"A few days for you," said Scarlett. "This case has lasted a little bit longer than that for me. A lot has changed over that time. For all of us." I didn't know what her look meant, and I wasn't sure I wanted to know.

"So why do you need me?"

"I wish I could tell you everything, but I need to wrap up this Angus business first."

"Have you come back from the same time as Angus?"

"Not quite but close, I think. I've got an idea who sent him here. Care to comment on that, Eddie?"

There was no need to reply. She knew. From the smile, I could tell she knew that I had sent Angus. Maybe she even knew why.

"So, your name is Lauren," I said.

"Yes, but can we stick with Scarlett here? I'd like to hang on to some of my protocols. Besides, I prefer it."

"Who's Scarlett really?"

"No one important. A girl who had her identity borrowed."

"You mean *stolen*?"

"No. *Borrowed* is a more accurate description."

"What about Lauren? What's she like?"

"At this point in time, Lauren Bliss lives a normal life with her mother and father. I can safely say that she has never done anything remarkable until yesterday, when she ran away from home."

"Won't your parents worry?"

"Yes, but it doesn't matter. Every version created by an agent's jump is wiped away after use. The lines are only kept open as long as the investigation is ongoing."

"I don't get it. If the future you has taken over this body, where's the you from now?"

"Think of it as asleep at the back of my mind, unaware of what's going on but ready to wake up as soon as I jump out. If I were to jump back now, you'd be talking to a very confused girl indeed. The last thing she knew, she was at home in London. Now she is in Wellcome Valley, eating an extremely dry baked potato."

"That's a bit weird, isn't it?"

"I suppose." Scarlett took a bite of her potato. "But memory is a selective thing. Take this lunch. I try to change what I have each time when I'm in the same or a similar situation, but I won't remember the exact consistency of the potato. I might remember that it needed to be a bit warmer for the cheese to melt, but there's loads of stuff I won't recall. And what about all the other lunches, breakfasts, and dinners of my life? My memory will retain a few but discard the rest. Even at this age, there's lots your memory didn't think worth hanging on to. Imagine what it'll be like when you're older."

I had been so absorbed in our conversation that I hadn't noticed the table of girls watching us, until Scarlett took my hand, making them giggle and point.

"Look, Eddie, don't worry about this stuff. All that matters is what's happening now," she said. "That's what you learn doing this job."

I moved my hand away.

"Can I ask you one more thing?"

"I probably won't be able to answer it."

"Do we meet in the future?"

Her final smile was so full of sadness that I feared what she was going to say, but she sighed and replied, "I'm hoping we might meet again in the past."

CHAPTER 50

BEGINNING AT THE END

I DIDN'T CARE WHO I SAT NEXT TO IN ENGLISH THIS time. I was trying to make sense of everything, so Cornish's words washed over me until something he said struck a chord. "Mary Shelley begins her story not at the beginning but at the end."

"Why?" I demanded.

"Why what?" He looked confused.

"Isn't life confusing enough without jiggling around the order?"

I was aware of Angus and Scarlett watching me with interest.

"I mean, you don't go to a restaurant and ask for a pudding first, do you? They don't say who's won the football game before kickoff, do they? Bands don't play encores before they've even done one song."

"All valid points," said Cornish, "but Victor Frankenstein is telling his story in the past tense, which means it is something that has already happened, so by starting her story at the end, Mary Shelley—"

"It's not the end." It was Scarlett who interrupted this time.

"Would you care to expand on that?" said Cornish.

"The monster comes back, doesn't he?" said Scarlett. "In which case the book starts somewhere near the end, but not the very end."

Mr. Cornish spun around on his heel and threw his marker pen from one hand to the other. "That's true, although I wasn't going to mention that. I didn't want to spoil it for those of you who haven't read it yet."

Angus piped up next. "I thought that knowing what happens wasn't the same as knowing the story."

"True too, Angus," said Cornish, weaving his way between the desks, clearly enjoying the pace of the conversation. "The important thing is the words on the page."

"In which case it depends what version we're talking about," said Scarlett.

Cornish clapped his hands together excitedly. "Superb. Scarlett is talking about the two different versions of *Frankenstein*. The original was published in 1818, the second in 1831 when Mary Shelley revised the book. To answer your question, Scarlett, we'll be working from the revised text."

"I prefer the original," said Scarlett.

Cornish was momentarily caught off guard by this,

wrestling with an instinct to doubt that a student could possibly have not only read the book, but read the two different versions of it. "Why?" he asked.

"In the first one, Frankenstein makes his own decisions," she replied simply. "In the later one, he is the victim of fate."

"Really?" I had never seen Cornish look out of his depth before.

"Yes. Thirteen years on, Mary had buried three children and one husband. She had felt pain. She had lived through tragedy. She obviously found it easier to put her loss down to fate. She victimized herself, and so she allowed her most famous character to do the same."

"Very interesting," said Cornish. "Fate is certainly a key theme of the book that we'll be looking at. So, what do we think, comrades? Who here believes in fate?"

Hands went up. Mine stayed down. We were back on familiar ground, although I had changed my mind now. How could there be a fixed course of events if there were different futures, pasts, and presents? Nothing was certain. Even my memories had become slippery, uncertain things I could no longer rely on. I had never considered how large a hole my mother's death had left in my life until it was filled. I missed that emptiness. Without it, who was I?

After class, I walked out with Angus. He spoke to me out of the side of his mouth, managing to look much more suspicious than he would have looked speaking normally. "There's a plan."

"What kind of plan?"

He reached his hand into his pocket and handed me a packet of M&M's.

"Ah, a plan with sweets," I said. "My favorite kind."

Angus spoke seriously. "On the way home, you'll sit next to Scarlett. All you have to do is offer her an M&M and make sure she takes the blue one."

I flipped up the lid and saw a blue M&M at the top. "Why?"

We reached the car park and stepped out. "Look, this is your plan, Eddie. Not mine. I'm not asking you to trust me. I'm asking you to trust yourself. Give her the M&M. Don't give her the M&M. It's up to you, but you told me to tell you to do it."

I closed the packet and slipped it into my coat pocket.

"Last call for anywhere but here," yelled Bill.

"Never gets old," I said.

"He does," replied Angus. "Almost takes a whole bus full of kids over the edge. He loses his license after that."

Angus's mum flashed the car's headlights.

"Remember, Eddie, the blue sweet." Angus turned and ran to the car.

I got to the bus just as Bill was closing the doors. Scarlett was already there. I sat down next to her, then tried not to think about how close she was.

"How are you doing?" she asked.

"I feel like my brain has been tumble dried."

"Has Angus told you what he's doing here yet?"

"He says he's working for me."

"Yes."

"You knew, didn't you?"

"I guessed."

"Is it true?"

"The trouble with this business is that one minute you're talking to your best friend, the next it's your worst enemy," Scarlett said.

"Which are you?" Eddie asked.

"I'm someone trying to do a job. What did Angus give you?"

I took out the packet of M&M's. There was no point hiding anything from Scarlett. She took it, opened the top, and poured a few onto her palm, including the blue one.

"These are my favorite," she said. "Do you think I should have one?"

I shrugged.

"I especially like the look of the blue one."

"Angus told me to make you eat it," I admitted.

"Did he tell you what it would do to me?"

"No. What is it?"

"It contains some kind of temporal distortion reactor. The Echo Corporation has teams of echo jumpers who travel back to manufacture this stuff and hide it in the past so that it can be dug up and used."

"Used to do what?"

"There are two types that I'm aware of. Since *you* tried to give it to me, I hope it's a locator that returns the echo jumper to his or her originating point."

"What's the other type?"

Scarlett didn't answer. She gave me a pitying glance. "You remember what I asked you about Maguire? Often your instincts and intuition are all you've got to go on. As I told you, trust no one."

"Not even myself?"

"You've met Melody now. Is she how you expected her to be? Is your life what you expected it to be?"

"I don't know. She's not so different from how Ruby described her, I suppose."

"Melody Dane is a brilliant woman. It was she who inspired me to get involved with echo technology. I can't imagine what it was like for you, growing up in her shadow and under her influence. Can you?"

"Am I different in this version, then?"

"You're the same person, but your life is different." Scarlett poured the sweets back and handed the packet to me.

"You think the M&M would have hurt you?" I asked.

"The Eddie I know wouldn't hurt anyone," she replied.

"How much longer will this last?"

"It's almost over," she replied.

Bill slammed on the brakes.

"All right, Miss White. We're home. Good night."

"See you around, Eddie Dane."

I felt my chest tighten at the thought of her going, because each time she left I feared I would never see her again. When she got off, I stared out the window and watched her disappear into the darkness.

51

A PICTURE OF FRUSTRATION

I FOUND COMFORT IN RUBY'S PAINT-SPATTERED CHAOS, but I noticed how the painting on the easel was spikier than before. The colors were brighter and had been applied with more force.

"It's not regret," I said.

"No. It's frustration," she replied. She grinned at me and added, "Which, of course, means it's impossible to get right."

"Where's Melody?"

"Over at David's, teetering on the brink of the scientific discovery of the century."

"She will change the world," I said.

"I have no doubt about that," replied Ruby. "I have never had any doubts about that. Ever since she was a little girl, I knew Melody was going to change the world. My only doubt was whether she would change it for the better or the worse." Ruby raised her eyebrows to show she was trying to be funny.

"What about him?" I said.

"David? He's just David. He manages her, which is something."

"They think they can control time," I said. "That's what they're doing."

"Why would you want to?"

"To avoid making mistakes, I suppose?" I said.

"Life is mistakes, Eddie. Take you. You think you were planned? Not likely. But what a fine specimen of a mistake you are." She held up my chin, coloring it with orange paint. "Believe me, everything worthwhile begins life as a mistake."

"Then controlling time could help avoid making the same mistakes," I said.

"What's the point? You'll only end up making different ones."

"Do you think Melody would avoid having me if she could?"

"Who knows? But I tell you what I would do. I'd do everything the same."

"You're telling me you don't have any regrets?" I didn't try to hide the disbelief in my voice.

"Of course I have regrets, but I'd do it the same because that's what I'm like. Even if I tried to do things differently, they'd end up the same."

"How do you know?"

"Because I have tried to do things differently. Half my life was spent trying to be a better person, but you reach a certain age and you realize you don't have a choice about who you are. All of us are slaves to ourselves."

"You'd still have Melody, then?" I asked.

"Of course. If I didn't have her, I wouldn't have you, and while you're not exactly my first choice of living companion, you are you, and that's something."

Ruby plucked the paintbrush from the jar, wiped it clean with her fingertips, then dipped it in the paint to continue with the impossible task of finishing her picture of frustration.

CHAPTER 52

DEATH DROP POINT

MELODY DIDN'T COME HOME THAT EVENING. AS FAR AS I could tell, this wasn't especially unusual. Ruby suggested I call Maguire's number, which was written on a pad by the phone, if I was worried. I tried it but there was no answer. Outside, the weather was getting worse. I was feeling anxious because I felt like this world with Melody was going to be taken from me at any time. I considered cycling around, but Ruby told me it was too dangerous to go out on such a night, and I knew she was right, so I went upstairs to my room and stared at a blank wall until I fell asleep, only to be woken up by my mother's urgent whisper.

"Eddie. Get up. Now."

I opened my eyes. Melody loomed over the bed, her panicked face lit by the red glow of my bedside clock.

"What time is it?" I asked, rubbing my eyes.

"Late. You need to get up." She pulled my pillow from under my head.

"Why? What's going on?"

"I'll explain on the way. Downstairs in one minute."

She left my door open and went to her room. I saw the light go on and heard her hurriedly packing. I dressed as fast as I could, then joined her downstairs. As soon as she saw me, she opened the front door, revealing the dark storm that raged outside.

"Come on," she said.

I didn't move. "Not until I know why."

"Please, darling, do as you're told," she said through gritted teeth.

"No."

"I'm your mother. Do as you're told."

"No."

"Please, darling, we're in danger. We need to go."

"What about Ruby? We can't leave her."

"Your grandmother will be fine."

"What's happened?"

"I'll explain in the car." I realized that Maguire's car was parked outside.

"Is he in there?"

"No," she said. "I've borrowed his car."

"But you don't drive," I said.

"I can drive perfectly well. Now, please, get in the car."

When she touched my face, I could feel her hand trembling with fear.

I followed her to the car and got in. The engine was already running.

"I don't think we should be driving in this storm," I said.

"We have no choice." Melody threw her bag into the backseat and pulled out a book. It was her hardback copy of *Frankenstein*. "Read what's written at the back," she said.

"I know all this," I said. "I know about the random sentence. I don't get why it's fallen on the same night, since there are two of you working on it this time, but I know what's written because I've seen all this before."

Melody started the car. "I chose this book for our experiment because you and I were talking about it yesterday. The idea was to test whether the present could be affected by the past."

It took me a moment to realize that she hadn't listened to a word I said.

"Yes, I know, and it can," I said. "The sentence appears as if by magic."

"Read it," said Melody, still not listening.

I turned to the last page and read:

Do not trust David Maguire.

"I don't understand," I said. "Who wrote it?"

"It's my handwriting."

"So, you wrote it?"

"No, I went to the past and wrote a sentence I found in the book. When I returned, however, this was written there in its place. It's a warning from myself in the future, placed in that same moment in the past for me to read now."

Melody switched the windscreen wipers to full speed, but they were losing the battle against the torrential rain.

"Did Maguire see it too?"

"He did. He kept trying to tell me it wasn't true, but I'm hardly going to trust him over myself, am I?"

On the more exposed stretches of road, I could feel the wind catching the car. It was a dreadful night to be out, but there was someone else on the road. Occasionally I could see the single headlight of a motorbike behind us. I didn't know if Melody had noticed.

"I need you to be brave, darling," she said.

"I'm not scared," I said. I threw the book onto the back-seat and spotted Maguire's shotgun.

"Why have you got his gun?" I asked.

Melody answered with her silence. For the first time, I noticed that her hands were stained with something dark and red.

"What have you done?"

"I needed to protect us," she said.

"What have you done?"

"Stop it, Eddie. Stop saying that."

My right hand closed around the packet of M&M's. I

pulled it out, flipped open the lid, and saw the blue one at the top. I could feel the roar of the engine as Melody pushed her foot down on the accelerator.

"You know I'd never do anything to harm you, darling," she said. "We're in this together. No matter what, we're in this together, you and me."

Melody made no attempt to slow down for the corner, and at the speed she was going, the skid was inevitable. Her hands twitched, turning the wheel to regain control of the car. She was gripping it so tightly that I could see the blue veins in her hands.

The next corner was even sharper and she was going even faster. We never stood a chance. I didn't try to grab the wheel. Or yell. I simply tipped the packet of sweets into my mouth as we hit the barrier and bit into the blue one. It tasted bitter and everything slowed down. I saw the fear and panic in my mother's eyes. In the rearview mirror, I saw the motorbike stop on the road. The items on the backseat flew into the air. I viewed these things with curiosity as the car shot off the road at the corner that I knew would one day be named Death Drop Point.

53

THE END OF EDDIE DANE

DURING HER TIME IN THE COURTROOM, LIPHOOK HAD come to realize that everything she had done in her life was for nothing. None of it meant anything. Her world was not an originating timeline. She, and everyone she had ever known, had lived life in an echo.

As soon as she returned home she felt her memories running away from her. At first, she believed it was some kind of side effect of the echo jump, but it was more than that.

Everything was coming to an end. She thought back on her life. After the incident at Maguire's farmhouse, she had left Wellcome Valley for a job in the big city, finally finding all the excitement and danger she had desired. She had the scars, the aches, and the pains to prove it. She had achieved everything she had set out to do, but now, with her career behind her, she realized that the one thing she had failed to achieve was companionship.

Liphook was alone.

Alone except for her memories.

She recalled with fondness the arrival of the Sandlings that night at the hospital. Angus's large family had breathed new life into the stagnant waiting room. In spite of the noise, both Liphook and Ruby were grateful for the distraction. Angus's twin brothers were incapable of doing anything other than bickering and winding each other up, but it was preferable to the anxious silence that had filled the room before. Ruby found comfort holding the baby, while Liphook reflected on how a large family brought with it an environment of its own that cushioned those inside from any horrors the world could throw at them.

It was a night of unrelenting atrocities. The news that Angus was very likely to spend the rest of his life in a wheelchair was utterly devastating for the family. Liphook wished she could do something to alleviate their pain.

In contrast to Angus's large family, Ruby was alone in her torture.

At one minute past midnight, a young male doctor, who looked as tired as Liphook felt, came into the waiting room. From the expression on his face, it was not going to be good news.

"Please, have a seat," he said to Ruby.

"I'm fine standing," she replied. Liphook placed her arm around Ruby's shoulders.

He nodded gravely. "I'm so very sorry," he said. "Your grandson has passed away."

Liphook felt all of Ruby's strength vanish. She went limp and would have collapsed to the ground had Liphook not been there to lower her gently onto a seat.

The doctor explained that Eddie had died peacefully in his sleep and, as far as he could tell, had felt no pain, but the words didn't even touch the surface of Ruby's grief. The Sandlings offered kind words of condolence, but all Liphook could offer was an arm and shoulder as Ruby wept for her grandson.

"They're not for me," Ruby said eventually. "These tears. They're for him. That poor kid got lumped with me his whole life. He got stuck in this valley with me. I thought that if I could get him through this bit of his life, then he could go off and do whatever he wanted, but if it's over now, it means he spent his whole life waiting for his life to start. What a waste. What an unforgivable, disgusting waste."

"You can't blame yourself," said Liphook.

"I told you, it's not about me. It doesn't matter who I blame. I used to say to him that maybe we would do better in the next life, but I never believed that. You only get one go at this. Except that poor lad lying dead on that slab never even got that. Regret is the worst."

Liphook had always valued her memories, but a memory could not outlive the mind that held it, and now everyone's memories were being destroyed. The world she had known was being annihilated. Every single thing was going to be scratched out and restarted.

54

ECHO
FREE-FALLING

"ECHO FREE-FALLING CAN OCCUR FOR A NUMBER OF reasons but is most often the result of the death of an individual in a previously inhabited version. This leaves your conscious self untethered and lost. If this should happen to you, you will find yourself pinballing forward and backward through time, crisscrossing versions of reality. In this event, it is vital that you stay calm and remain at the background of each host mind. The further forward you push yourself, the more difficult it will be for our experts to extract you."

I didn't know who was speaking, only that it was a calm voice that reminded me of a safety announcement. The next thing I heard was my own voice.

"You're sure you won't have a dessert? It's on me." The voice sounded deeper, but I knew it was mine because I heard it from inside my head.

Looking out of my eyes, I saw that I was sitting in a fancy restaurant. Angus was opposite me. His hairline was farther back and there were lines around his eyes and mouth. Apart from that, he was just the same.

"Why me?" he said. "I don't understand why you're asking me, Eddie."

"Because I know you like dessert and they've got a great selection here."

He gave me a withering look.

"Because you're my friend, Angus," I said. Apparently I knew what he was really referring to. "And because you're not involved in all this and because I trust you. There aren't many people I do now."

Watching this from the back of my head, I was a spectator to my own thoughts as they crossed my mind.

"I can't be bought," said Angus. "I'm not for sale."

"I'm not trying to buy you. I'm asking you for help and offering what I can in return."

"Do you remember the project?" said Angus. "The ten tallest trees in the valley?"

I felt the contractions in my cheeks as I smiled. "I never even liked climbing trees. I only did it because you did."

"I knew that," said Angus. "I was grateful. It was always more fun with you."

A waitress placed cups of coffee in front of us. Angus thanked her and took a sip, but I didn't say anything. I poured milk from a small jug into my cup and watched it color the coffee.

"Do we have to go through all this again?" I recognized the tightening sensation in my chest as guilt, although I didn't understand what I felt guilty about.

"Isn't that what you're asking me to do? Go over things again?" he said.

I leaned forward and spoke quietly. "Things have changed. The technology has moved on. It's now possible for you to go back and start again. You can live your life over. You can do things differently."

"I thought all jump cords had to be cut."

"There are ways around that. I could arrange it for you."

"Thanks, but I'm happy with my life."

I snorted into my coffee in disbelief. I hated myself for doing it.

"I know I'm not rich like you," said Angus, "but I am happy, Eddie. I never blamed you for what happened. I knew it was my own fault, but when Melody made all that money and you left the valley and stopped calling, it wasn't that I resented you for going. It was just . . ." He trailed off for a moment. "When I was lying there, waiting to be found, unable to move, in all kinds of agony, I wished so much that you were there. Not to go get help, not because you'd probably have stopped me from climbing so high, but because I knew you'd be able to make me laugh. It's been years since I laughed like we used to."

"Things aren't as funny these days," I said.

"Last call for anywhere but here," said Angus.

"I'm not here for a trip down memory lane," I said harshly.

"I thought that was exactly why you asked me here."

"You know what I mean. I need your help to stop Maguire before he wipes her from history."

"I don't even understand half of this. I've never had any interest in that echo stuff."

"I know, which means they won't suspect you. The ETA is in Maguire's pocket. We're running out of time."

"The ETA?" Angus nodded knowingly. I could tell this annoyed me, but I wasn't clear why.

I could feel a hundred different emotions wrestling inside of me.

"How is she?" asked Angus.

"Tenacious," I said.

I realized we were talking about Scarlett.

"I'm sorry things didn't work out with you two," said Angus. "I liked her."

"It's history," I said dismissively, but from the turmoil in my head I doubted this was true.

"What isn't history these days?" said Angus.

This brought my anger and frustration into focus. "Will you do it? It's not hard, what I'm asking. You'll receive full instructions that will help us stop the ETA from meddling and letting Maguire clear his name."

"By *us*, you mean you and Melody?"

"I need to protect her."

"I'll do it, but for you. Not for her," said Angus.

"Thank you."

"I'm agreeing to help because we used to be friends, and that still means something to me."

"I hope we're still friends," I said.

"Listen, Eddie, thanks for lunch. It wasn't quite Thursday meatballs, but it was nice."

"I'll send someone to pick you up in the morning," I said.

Angus placed his hands on the table and pushed. I was expecting him to stand and was surprised when he slid back. I watched him navigate his wheelchair through the crowded restaurant. He never once looked back.

I felt the weight of every dark thought in my head. I witnessed my own fear and determination. I was using Angus. I was sending him to do something I was too scared to do myself. I watched myself dismiss this guilt. I had promised Melody I would carry out her plan. I had to protect my mother. That was all that mattered to me.

55

MANIPULATION

THE FEELING OF WEIGHTLESSNESS WAS LOST AS I found myself in a room that was unfamiliar to me, and yet I knew I had been here many times. I was on my feet. My mother stood at a darkened window that went all the way down to the shiny floor. She had her back to me and was looking down at the city lights.

"The trial is approaching the end," I said.

"Then it is important that we don't take any more risks. This must go our way, not Maguire's."

"Maguire has been brought in now," I said. "He's given evidence but refused to clarify either way what happened."

"Of course he refused to talk," snapped my mother, turning around to face me, revealing the anger in her eyes. "Murderers don't give themselves up."

"I suppose not," I said. Doubt crossed my mind. I watched my host body dismiss it.

"Eddie, darling," said my mother, "I know this is hard, but we have to take these matters into our own hands. If we leave it to the ETA, David will turn things his way. I don't understand the game he's playing, but I do know the goal he has in mind. He wants to destroy all this."

She waved her hands in the air.

"I know," I said, "but the ETA isn't working for him anymore."

My mother smiled. "It's her, isn't it? It's Lauren. You have to realize that your marriage is over now. She'll help *him*, not us."

"I don't think that's true," I said. "Not about our marriage, I know that's over, but Lauren is only trying to do the right thing."

"You say that like there's only one right thing. Everyone has their own version of what is right, but you and I, Eddie, we know the truth—and the truth is that David wants to get rid of me. From this and every version. He wants to live in a world of his own design."

"But Lauren will discover the truth . . ."

"She'll discover the version of the truth she's looking for, and that could too easily be one without me. She never liked me. You know she didn't. This is personal."

"I don't think she would—"

"You never think anything bad about her," interrupted my mother. "It's always been up to me to point out what her real motives were in marrying you. I'm the only one who has your best interests at heart, and you're the only one who has mine. Right now, do you know where she is?"

"No. Probably at the agency, gathering evidence."

"She's echo jumping. She's back at the discovery stage, manipulating the situation. She's planning to use another version of you, Eddie, to get the result they want. She's *using* you, Eddie. We need to stop her."

"Stop her how?"

My mother held out her hand. In her palm was a single blue pill.

"I won't do anything to hurt her," I said.

"This won't hurt her. It's a tracker. It will send her back to our present before she manages to finish what she's doing. All new echo jumps have been suspended, so she won't be able to go back again."

"You promise?" I said.

"Eddie, darling, I'm not a monster." She raised her hand to my cheek, and I felt so many emotions that I could barely distinguish what was what, except that this host body, inside which I was hiding, would have done anything for this woman. "You can't go yourself. They're watching us. You need to find someone you trust."

"I'm not sure I trust anyone anymore."

"Find someone to help us. Someone not involved. Someone you can manipulate. Do it quickly, or we'll lose everything we've worked for."

In my mind's eye, I pictured Angus. *Yes*, I heard myself think, *I'll get Angus to do it.*

CHAPTER 56

THE END OF
THE WORLD

THERE WAS NO RUSHING WIND OR LURCHING SENSA-
tion in my stomach, but it did feel as helpless and hopeless
as falling. Days passed like seconds. All my lives flashed
before my ever-changing eyes, hinting at all the possibilities and impossibilities of every decision. I caught glimpses
of how my life would have been with a mother. Her expectations. Her disappointment. My desire to please her. My
unconditional love for her, no matter what she did or what
she asked me to do.

I saw Ruby refusing to admit she was growing old until
her fingers could no longer grip a paintbrush. I saw her
alone, unable to look after herself. I saw her screaming
and crying when I came to take her from her home. I wrestled with her and pushed back my emotions.

I saw Scarlett, young and old, happy and sad, angry

and disappointed, laughing uncontrollably and weeping inconsolably. I couldn't make sense of it all, but what I did understand was so painful that I was relieved when it stopped and I found myself standing in a crowded room, once again tucked away at the back of my mind.

At the front of the room, behind a small stage, was a logo with an arrow curving around to form a globe with the letters *ETA* written below. A man in a gray suit stood onstage, urging everyone to sit down. I found a seat. The man next to me was fiddling with his watch.

"Another day, another announcement from the ETA," he said. He pressed a button on his watch and it projected various computer icons above his wrist. "Blasted thing. Never works when I need it." He switched it off and took out a pad and pen. "Much easier," he said.

I waited to hear my reply but none came.

At the back of the room, cameramen and journalists jostled for position. "Any idea what this one's about?" asked the man next to me.

"I have my suspicions," I said.

The man turned to look at me. "Hey, don't I recognize you?"

"Look, it's starting now," I said.

The man onstage tapped the microphone on the lectern and spoke. "Ladies and gentlemen of the press, please welcome senior echo time agent Lauren Bliss."

Scarlett walked out onto the stage, exuding confidence and authority. She was blond and she looked older, but no less beautiful in a blue uniform with the same logo of the curved arrow.

"Ladies and gentlemen of the press, thank you for coming."

The room fell quiet. "I know many of you will be pressed for time," she began.

"Unlike you lot," shouted a journalist at the back, winning a small, halfhearted pocket of laughter.

"There will be an opportunity for questions and attempts at humor at the end," said Scarlett, getting a much better response. "This announcement concerns the planned action following the decision to eradicate all remaining altered versions."

An excited murmur spread through the room.

"About time too," the man next to me muttered.

"It is not a decision we at the ETA take lightly," said Scarlett. "The consequences of what we are about to do will have ramifications far beyond this version of existence."

"In English, please," shouted the loudmouthed journalist at the back.

"She's talking about the end of the world," responded another.

Scarlett smiled. "In spite of your glib tabloid summary, you're not far off. We are talking about the end of all altered versions of existence," she said. "As you know, it has been law for well over a decade that all new versions created for whatever reason must be destroyed after use. However, this new decision requires us to go back and delete all versions created before this law."

"Good thing too," said the man next to me. From the mutterings of approval, this appeared to be the sentiment of most of the room.

"That's right," said a snooty-sounding woman at the side of the room. "Professor Maguire's own report warned of dangers of temporal erosion caused by the existence of too many timelines."

"The report cited this as a possibility, not a reality," said Scarlett. "But whatever the truth of the dangers, it has been decided that it is not a risk worth taking, so the ETA will now embark on a series of investigations to determine which versions have been altered and which is the originating version."

"So, the end of the world, then," yelled the same journalist as before.

Scarlett had to fight to regain the attention of the room. "It is for this very reason that Professor David Maguire has resigned his post as chief adviser to the ETA."

"What about the rumors that Maguire has created his own personal altered version with no Melody Dane?" said the snooty journalist.

"I cannot comment on ongoing cases and investigations within the ETA," said Scarlett. "Nor am I here to answer for Professor Maguire."

"Will he be holding a press conference too?" yelled another voice.

"As soon as Professor Maguire is located, the ETA will be issuing a statement."

Given the strong reaction this got, it was odd that my own mind was extremely calm. Apparently I was not surprised by anything I had heard so far.

"He's gone missing?" said the man next to me.

"Run away, has he?" shouted the loudmouth.

"I am unable to comment on Professor Maguire's whereabouts at this time. All I can tell you is that, as an outspoken critic of this policy, he has found his own position as chief adviser to the ETA untenable and so has stepped down."

"And run off to hide in a world where he can get what he wants," said the snooty woman.

"The consequence of this policy will make it impossible for anyone to hide in altered versions," said Scarlett.

"In English, please."

"It's the end of every world except one," she replied, for the first time catching my eye.

CHAPTER 57

FINAL CHIPS

SEEING SCARLETT'S FACE SO NEAR TO MINE, IT TOOK ME a moment to recognize our surroundings. The clatter of the cutlery and the smell of the food brought me to my senses. I looked down at the plate of chips on my tray. At a nearby table, a group of girls pretended not to watch us. We were back in the school hall. Everything was as before except this time, Scarlett had chips. She picked one up, dipped it in ketchup, and took a bite.

"It's all right to speak," she said.

"To say what?" I replied.

"You have every reason to be upset," she said. "I can't imagine what you've been through."

"Which version are we in now?" I asked.

"This is a temporary moment that will be destroyed as soon as we leave. You've been stabilized now. It's almost over."

"What happened to me?"

"You were echo free-falling," said Scarlett. "You heard the announcement, didn't you?"

"The one that told me I was dead and to remain calm?" I said.

"Yes," she replied. "It turns out that blue M&M was nastier than I thought. It did locate your originating point, but it didn't send you back. It sent you into cardiac arrest. It killed your originating self."

"So, I'm dead?"

"Dead men don't eat chips, Eddie, but it was touch and go for a while. Luckily for you, your originating consciousness was already in an altered version."

"The one created by Cornish's illegal echo jump?"

"And mine. Remember, I jumped in too."

"What?"

"Don't hurt yourself trying to understand every detail. Just know that in spite of your best efforts, you are still alive."

"But I told Angus to give it to you."

"Did you know what it would do?"

"No, I don't think so. Maybe. I'm not sure. I was trying to protect Melody." I paused and looked down at the blob of ketchup on my plate. "Scarlett, am I the bad guy?"

She squeezed my hand. "It doesn't matter. You're going to make up for all this. This you is going to make things right."

"I want to see Ruby."

"You'll see her soon."

"I want to go home."

"The whole world is going home now. We're starting again." She picked up another chip. "You know, I wish I'd gone for chips the first time. Most field agents pig out when they echo jump, but I had this crazy idea that I should try to stay healthy. Stupid, really."

"I don't get it," I said. "Has everything I've just seen already happened?"

"It has, but it won't have soon. All those futures are being destroyed and all those pasts are being tidied up."

"So, everything will make sense?"

"I don't think you can assume that. Things don't make sense. Not really. The world isn't fair. You can try all you like to make it so, but someone will always find a loophole. Even now that they want to clean everything up, I doubt it will stay like that."

"How many versions are there left?"

"Not taking into account this temporary branch, there are two, and it's time to call the final witness. You."

"Why me? What have I witnessed?"

"I need you to do one last jump back to the first point of divergence."

"Melody's death," I said.

Scarlett nodded. "That's where all these investigations have led. Maguire stands on trial for her murder. We need your testimony."

"Why me?"

"Because you were there, Eddie. You can't remember it, but you witnessed Melody's death. If we sent anyone else back, their presence would be too likely to affect the outcome."

"Can't you just hypnotize me to remember?"

"No. We need to be sure. Believe me, this was my last resort. Sending you back that far is not without its dangers. You'll be entering your infant mind, opening up the danger of overworking it and causing mental damage. You'll also be reliving a memory you have suppressed for a very good reason."

"Will I be able to speak?"

"No, your vocal cords won't be developed enough. Even if you could, a talking baby would be enough to make anyone crash a car." Scarlett's smile was the emptiest I had ever seen it.

"So, what can I do?"

"Listen and watch."

Scarlett placed her hand on top of mine. The group of girls giggled, but at that moment, I could not have cared less. "So, no one will remember this," I said.

"That's right," she replied.

I leaned over the table and kissed her. Her lips were so soft that it felt as though the world was melting. Then it did.

58

THURSEABER

I ENTERED A MEMORY FROM BEFORE I KNEW WHAT memory was. I was shuffling and struggling. My mind was awash with confused, wordless emotions. It was dark and something was hurting my shoulders. My mother stood over me. She looked like she did in the photograph, although I knew her more by smell than sight. She finished fiddling with the two strong straps holding me down, and I felt the buckle pinch my thigh. When I cried out in pain, I heard the shrill shriek of a baby.

"Look, I'm sorry, darling," said my mother, "but if you didn't make such a fuss, you wouldn't get hurt, would you?"

"Where are you taking him?" Ruby was standing behind my mother. The rain came down hard on her uncovered head.

"Go back inside, woman," said Melody.

"At least wait until it stops raining. It's not safe to drive in this."

"He's safer with me than with you," replied Melody.

"You're overreacting. Everyone leaves their door unlocked around here."

"Not when they're supposed to be looking after their grandson. You had that music up so loud you couldn't even hear him crying."

"I can hear him crying now," said Ruby pointedly. "You'll only be back. You need my help. You never have any time for the lad."

"I wouldn't expect you to understand," yelled Melody. "David and I are working on something very important."

"More important than your child?"

"The child has nothing to do with David. He's mine. Do you understand? Mine."

"The child has a name," said Ruby.

Melody slammed the car door shut, so I couldn't hear what was said next, but Melody was soon sitting in the driver's seat, turning the key. She tried the seat belt but it didn't come out, so she gave up and put the car into gear. I had to warn her.

"Thurseaber," I managed to say. My tongue felt swollen and oversized in my infant mouth.

"Don't worry, darling. Everything's going to be all right."

Out the window, I could see Ruby standing in the doorway. The rain on the car roof sounded like thunder. The car moved and I felt a wave of drowsiness. I fought to stay awake. "Thurseaber, thurseaber," I muttered.

"Quiet down now, darling."

She leaned over and fumbled with her bag, causing the car to swerve. She got it back under control and pulled out her mobile phone. With her left thumb, she dialed a number, then clicked it onto speakerphone.

"Hello?" It was Maguire's voice. "Melody? Where are you? What's wrong?"

"I'm leaving," she replied.

"Come on, don't get like this over a little argument."

"You called me an unfit mother."

"I didn't mean it like that. It was you who said the baby was getting in the way of our work."

"Thurseaber," I screamed.

"Please, darling, give it a rest," yelled Melody.

"What's going on?" said Maguire. "Are you driving?"

"It's not your concern."

"It is my car, though, isn't it? You shouldn't be driving in weather like this. Please, come around and we can talk about it."

"There's nothing to talk about. We're leaving. We're getting out of this godforsaken place. I'm going to start over."

"And throw away everything we're trying to do?" said Maguire.

"I wouldn't be throwing away anything. I am perfectly capable of completing the project with or without you."

"I've given up everything for this," said Maguire.

"So have I."

"What did you have to give up?"

"Good-bye, David."

My mother only looked down to disconnect the call, but it was long enough. We had reached the corner. I felt the skid of the wheel. I heard screaming, although I don't know whether it was her, me, or the sound of the brakes. As the car flew off the road, my mother shot out of her seat and went straight through the windscreen. I felt moisture spatter my skin, but I didn't know if it was blood or rain.

59

THE TESTIMONY OF MR. EDWARD DANE

"THE COURT WILL NOW HEAR THE TESTIMONY OF MR. Edward Dane."

The judge sat up high in the courtroom. Scarlett was standing in front of me, wearing the same uniform as before. My mother was next to a man I didn't recognize. Maguire was in another box across the room from me. The rest of the large room was filled with people. Most were strangers, but some were familiar from the press conference. Everyone looked older. They were all staring at me.

"Are you ready to testify, Eddie?" asked Scarlett.

"What?" I was gazing at my hands. A moment ago, they had been those of an infant. Now they were the hands of a man. I looked for a mirror to check my reflection. Instead, I spotted a pair of eyes I recognized. PC Liphook was sitting in the front row. She was an old woman now. I refused to allow myself to think about why Ruby was not present.

"The witness seems a bit disoriented," said the judge.

"With respect, Your Honor," said Scarlett, "Eddie has been echo free-falling since the death of a previously inhabited version of himself. As well as seeing countless glimpses of his own future, he has just sat helplessly and watched his mother's death. It would be more surprising if he were not disoriented."

"Is that correct, Mr. Dane?" said the judge. "Did you just witness the death of Melody Dane?"

I nodded.

"Let the record show that the witness nodded," said the judge.

There was whispered excitement from the courtroom. The judge silenced the room with a look. "Thus far, we have heard from many witnesses in this trial, most of whom have secured the destruction of what they believed to be the true version of events." I saw the judge look at Liphook and then turn back to Scarlett. "Now it is our time to learn the truth about our own."

"Please, in your own time, Eddie, tell us what you saw," said Scarlett.

"It was raining," I said. "My mother was arguing with Ruby."

"You're referring to Ruby Dane, your grandmother?" said Scarlett.

"She doesn't like the G-word," I said.

"What were they arguing about?" asked the judge.

"Ruby had left the door unlocked while she was looking after me or something."

"May I ask the relevance of this?" said the man next to my mother.

"I think we all want as clear a view of the events as possible," said the judge, "so please hold back any questions until the end of the testimony." He turned back to me. "Please continue, but bear in mind that you are under oath and that the consequences of your testimony will have serious ramifications . . . for everyone."

I looked at my mother, trying to read her expression. Something lurked behind her eyes, but I couldn't tell if it was fear, anger, or something else. All my life, she had been nothing more than an echo of a whispered word. In reality, she was much more complex than that, so much darker and brighter than I could have ever imagined.

"Maguire is innocent," I said. "He didn't kill her. It was an accident. Melody made a phone call while driving without a seat belt. That's why she died."

The courtroom fell quiet except for Melody, who was urgently whispering to the man next to her.

"Melody, I understand," I said. "I always felt cheated too. I felt wronged. I wanted someone to blame, but it was just a stupid accident. It was nothing."

"To be clear," said Scarlett, "are you saying that David

Maguire did not play any part in the death of Melody Dane?"

"Yes," I said.

The judge had to bring his gavel down several times to silence the courtroom. Maguire summoned Scarlett over. He spoke hurriedly to her, and then, once order had been regained, she said, "In view of this evidence, Professor Maguire would like to alter his statement."

"You have something to say, Professor Maguire?" said the judge.

Maguire stood up, glanced at me, then addressed the judge. "Melody Dane was my friend," he said. "I never cared whether the child was mine, but I did care about her. Together Melody and I shared a common pursuit. We shared a dream. We knew we would change the world, but the world had other ideas. It removed her from that equation. So when I discovered it was possible to alter the past, Melody was my first thought. If it was possible to change the world's mistakes, I would correct that one. I went back and stopped her from dying."

"How?" asked the judge.

"I sold my car," replied Maguire.

"And what had happened when you arrived back from the jump?" inquired the judge.

"She was alive. She never died."

"But that means that ours is not the originating version," said the judge.

"That is correct," said Maguire. "This policy has always been suicidal because it was decided in a world created when I saved Melody. Many believe that all these versions are awfully messy, but life is messy. It is messy and chaotic and strange and, as far as I'm concerned, endlessly wondrous. When I saved Melody's life, I was correcting an accident that should never have happened."

"He's lying," yelled Melody. The man next to her tugged her sleeve and urged her to sit down, but there was no containing her anger. "You've got it the wrong way around. You can't believe his testimony over mine. This witness has been manipulated by the ETA agent. David Maguire is a murderer. *This* is the originating version."

"Silence," shouted the judge forcefully.

Melody sat back down.

"Melody Dane, it was you who began these proceedings. When you learned of a version without you, you assumed that it was the result of foul play. You never considered that it could be the originating version. Would you have ever begun this if you had, I wonder? But now that we have had to face this question, you must accept the conclusion of this trial. We all must."

"I'll never accept it," said Melody.

Maguire addressed her as though they were the only two people in the room. "I never accepted it either," he said. "You deserved life. You deserved everything you have achieved. The Echo Corporation is not what I would have done, but it was what you wanted. You always had more business sense and ambition than me. I'm glad I helped you realize your dream."

"But, Professor Maguire," said the judge, "you stood here accused of murder when, in fact, we've just heard that you had saved the life you were accused of taking. Why would you not use this as your defense from the start?"

"If I had told the truth, then this version would have been destroyed. Melody would have been killed a second time. I never wanted that. I still don't want that."

Even the judge was unable to reclaim the courtroom after this, so he announced that the court was in recess while a verdict was being reached.

The only people not talking were Melody and Maguire, who were staring at each other in silent dismay.

"Well done, Eddie," said Scarlett. "I know it can't have been easy."

"What happens now?" I asked. "What happens to me?"

"The same thing that will happen to all of us. The time-line will be cleaned up. No more multiple versions of the world. Everything we have achieved and all the mistakes we've made are going to be wiped away. A new originating point will be picked. Procedures will be put into place to prevent this from happening again. That's the idea."

"But how can that be possible if—"

"Eddie," she interrupted, "the only thing you need to know is that the world is going back to square one."

"But then won't it all just happen again?"

"Who knows? They think they have a plan in place to ensure it doesn't, but you just heard Maguire. The man who changed the world to save the woman he loved, only to have her accuse him of murder, has no regrets."

"Will I remember any of this?" I said.

"The idea is that none of us will," she replied, "but I don't know if that's true. You've echo jumped enough now to understand that versions aren't as neatly compartmentalized as we think. They bleed into each other. You have experienced time slippage when you see things you have never experienced and you remember things that never happened to you. Who is to say we won't remember some of this? Let's try, shall we?"

"But what should we remember?"

"That's up to you." She took my hand in hers. I felt the warmth of her skin. "But me? I'm going to try to remember the day we first met."

"That rainy day on the bus?" I said.

"No. Before that. My reality. It was a sunny day in the valley. I was on holiday. I was lost. You found me."

Her words ignited a fire in the back of my mind, like something halfway between a memory and a daydream. "Will we meet again?" I asked.

"We already have," she replied.

60

THE BEGINNING

IT WAS THE SUMMER HOLIDAYS AND I WAS CYCLING around on my own, going nowhere in particular, when I first saw Lauren. It was one of those rare moments, among all those gray rainy days in the valley, when the sun shines and you realize how far you can see. The sky was endless blue, the valley was a hundred shades of green, and there she was, running through a field of yellow sunflowers.

So many colors, but not one that compared with her.

She was waving her arms and running toward a police car that had just overtaken me. The female police officer smiled at me as she passed, but she can't have heard the girl shouting because she didn't slow down and her car disappeared around the corner.

I stopped my bike and stared at the girl. I suppose I must have felt invisible, because I was surprised when she saw me.

"Hello? Excuse me. Can you help? I'm lost," she said.

"I . . . er . . . I was just cycling past," I said stupidly. "Where are you trying to get to?"

"The cottage where I'm staying. We've just arrived. I'm here on holiday." She had green-blue eyes, which she rubbed with her fingertips.

"Are you staying in one of the holiday cottages?" I asked.

"Yes, but I can't remember what it's called."

I laughed.

"I know. It's stupid. I think it had something to do with honey. There are roses in the garden."

"That narrows it down."

Her smile was like nothing I had ever seen before and yet as familiar as though I had spent a hundred lifetimes basking in its warmth.

"I'm Lauren," she said.

"Eddie," I replied. "I'll help you find your cottage if you like."

"Thanks. I was beginning to worry that I'd be searching all night and end up getting eaten by wolves."

"Well, we haven't found it yet . . . You still might," I replied. "Except we don't have wolves here. It's more likely you'll get nibbled to death by sheep."

We set off down the road. It was strange how easy she was to talk to, but I didn't question it.

I stopped walking.

"What is it?" she said.

"Shout something," I replied.

"Like what?"

"Anything."

At the top of her voice, she shouted, "Anything!"

The word bounced off the hills and came back to us.

"Cool echo," she said. "It's like there's another me shouting back."

"There isn't much to do around here. Talking to yourself is the best entertainment we've got."

"I like it," she said. "Are you on holiday here too?"

"No, I live here."

"Wow."

Even though I normally hated life in the valley, today I understood what she meant. At that moment it looked like the most stunning place on earth.

"It's not normally like this," I said. "This is a good day."

"Yes, it is," she replied.

NOTES ON THE US VERSION OF
NO TRUE ECHO

WHEN I WRITE A BOOK, I INEVITABLY CREATE COUNTLESS different versions of the same story. Each draft takes me further from the originating version and closer to the altered version you have just read. The UK version of this book was created with the help of the following echo agents: Lisa Whittaker, Leslie Jones, Lesley Jones, Naomi Colthurst, Sarah Odedina, and Melissa Hyder. This US version involved further input from Richard Slovak, Susan Van Metre, and Erica Finkel. Then there is you, the reader. I cannot say what expectations, understanding, and interpretations you brought to this story, but it is my belief that no story exists in just one version.

I only hope that you enjoyed your version of this one.

Any questions?